LIVING
FOREVER

LIVING FOREVER

— *a novel* —

JAN FAWCETT

iUniverse, Inc.
Bloomington

Living Forever

This is a work of fiction. All of the characters, names, incidents, organizations, and dialogue in this novel are either the products of the author's imagination or are used fictitiously.

iUniverse books may be ordered through booksellers or by contacting:

iUniverse
1663 Liberty Drive
Bloomington, IN 47403
www.iuniverse.com
1-800-Authors (1-800-288-4677)

ISBN: 978-1-4759-8459-0 (sc)
ISBN: 978-1-4759-8460-6 (hc)
ISBN: 978-1-4759-8461-3 (e)

Library of Congress Control Number: 2013906178

Printed in the United States of America

iUniverse rev. date: 05/15/2013

To my love and my muse, Katie Busch, who has totally supported me in my career and creative endeavors. To my children, Robin Fawcett, Holly Fawcett, Marc Fawcett, and Andrea Fawcett, as well as the memory of my deceased son, Craig Fawcett, who "marched to the beat of a different drummer." Also to my grandchildren, Jessica, Brittany, Jameson, and Marshall.

Acknowledgments

My struggle to express thoughts and questions about life required help from others. In trying to get *Living Forever* into a readable form, I was helped by people who were willing to read my drafts and make constructive comments. Interestingly, many of the comments and criticisms were different from individual to individual, while some converged. They were all very helpful.

I could not have even begun this quest without the help, the teaching, and especially the encouragement from my writing coach, Julie Mars. I must thank Mary Ann Liebert, who read my early (somewhat bloated) draft three times and made very constructive comments, which I heeded. I also thank her for her sage advice as a successful publisher. I thank Richard Lam for reading and advising me on the draft. My son Marc Fawcett deserves my sincere appreciation for reading through a draft and making an honest and helpful critique.

Dick and Joy Brams deserve my special thanks for their thoughtful review and comments after reviewing this work several times and for making helpful suggestions.

I thank Sandy Finkel, MD, for his critique, and I must especially thank Rhona Finkel for her line-by-line review of the draft and particularly for her honest comments about content. Her input and efforts were very helpful. Friends, too numerous to recount, have discussed the ideas in this book with me and have encouraged my writing. My friends Robert Hirschfield, MD, Barry Altenberg, MD, and his wife, Michelle, and my daughter Andrea Fawcett also read drafts and made helpful comments. My granddaughter Jessica Fawcett-Patel provided much-needed technical help in generating this manuscript.

People can express true love in many ways. Encouraging creativity in one's mate is one of the highest forms of the expression of love. I could not have finished this effort without the help of Katie Busch, my soul mate, muse, and supportive critic, who not only read the story aloud to me (what a revelation that was—redundancy that I had totally missed smacked me across the face) but also did a thoughtful line-by-line review. Her support and interest helped me persist, draft after draft.

So the journey is winding down, and here is *Living Forever*. I thank any readers for the investment of their precious time and hope that reading this book adds to their consciousness.

Thus shall ye think of this fleeting world:

a star at dawn.

a bubble in a stream,

a flash of lightning in a summer cloud,

a flickering lamp,

a phantom,

and

a dream.

—Vajracchedika Prajnaparamita Sutra

Thanks to Sunyata, 1990

Chapter 1

LOOKING BACK

Before his life splintered into chaos, Ian Farrell experienced a momentary encounter in a mirror. It began as a check for the completeness of his shave or the possible need for a haircut and progressed to a rare internal conversation about the state of his life and future.

His drooping eyelids provoked irritation along with the well-meant offer of his patient, a plastic surgeon suffering from depression, who'd caught him late on a long day and offered to eliminate the now redundant eyelids. *Do I look that old?* he wondered. He didn't *feel* sixty-eight, contrary to the mirror's truth.

He still loved skiing, despite needing to accept that his aging body could no longer handle the head-over-heels, arms-extended falls that occurred when he tried to snowboard. He remembered the day he had driven his young niece, visiting from college after growing up in Sun Valley, to the Santa Fe ski hill, skis sticking out the back of the open convertible. It hadn't mattered that, later, he couldn't keep up with her. The majesty of skiing down the mountain, rapidly, in full control, in the hushed quiet, still resonated. He had a zest and energy for life, creativity, curiosity, and even some sexual drive, when he could get enough sleep.

"I'm stretching middle age," he'd say when people remarked, "You don't look over fifty." He didn't feel old, but he sure ached in the morning. He tried to counter the inevitable loss of muscle mass by working out with his rowing machine. He also tried to keep up regular Zen meditation, but the days never afforded enough time.

How old, or young, am I? If I die tomorrow, I'm very old. If life goes on, I'm as young as I can feel.

Ian had learned from his medical career just how unpredictable and transient life is. He noticed how much of people's time was devoted to accumulating wealth to pay for constant material consumption. This focus on the business of living produced useless worry and fear that only detracted from experiencing life in the moment.

He looked down. *Damn! The back of my hand is bleeding! Another sign of aging,* he mused, *friable skin of my hands plus that daily aspirin.* The dark red blood droplets brought him into the present and led him to wonder if a struggle for life was going on between his immune cells and ravenous cancer cells in those drops of blood.

Suddenly aware of his self-preoccupation, he chided himself but then reflected, *It's not all that inappropriate, given tomorrow's scan to look for melanoma metastases—a death sentence.*

Caitlin had saved his life by hassling him to get a small, infected lesion on his chest checked. He knew it would run its course without need for a dermatologist, but he had given in to her. She did the worrying for both of them, since denial was his mantra in life. "What difference will it make in a hundred years?" was Ian's favorite justification for nonworry. "I'll go, but it'll be a waste of time for me and the doctor."

Dr. Persol, a dermatologist who always wore ties with dogs on them, said, "You're right. You didn't need to see me for this, but while you're here, we might as well do a total exam." Ian heard him breathing for a few seconds. "Hmmm. Look at this," he said as he positioned the mirror so Ian could see an ugly, flat, spreading melanoma of multiple colors.

The next day, Dr. Silk, with the enthusiasm of a young surgeon, cut it out with a big margin. "I think we got it all. You know, after a while, they start growing deeper, and if they get into the lymph channels, they really spread. I've arranged for you to follow up with Dr. Carlson in oncology."

Flash-forward a year to when Carlson had found enlarged lymph nodes in his left axilla, which required a workup.

He'd made his decision the moment that Caitlin and he had seen the clusters of black images under his left arm, in both lungs, and in his lumbar spine.

"Sorry, Ian. We should schedule a first course of chemotherapy as soon as we get the cell type." Dr. Carlson looked very serious.

Caitlin was clearly shaken and on the verge of tears. Her radiant smile was gone.

"Never worship a lab test," Ian countered.

He called Dr. Carlson's office, after it was closed, and left a message. He got Sampson to cover his patients and O'Brien to cover for the department. He packed that night and called the kids. He told them he was leaving on an emergency trip. They were used to that.

Ian planned to put the top down and head for the California beaches. "Maybe we can drive fast enough to keep up with the setting sun," he said.

"Dr. Carlson recommended chemotherapy, Ian," Caitlin protested. "Do you think there's any chance of it working?"

"I've reviewed the outcomes. Nothing's effective. The treatments just delay death by a few days, and like the chain-smoking comedian says, 'Who wants to live those extra days anyway?'" He reached for her hand. "A trip to the beach would be a much better use of our precious time. Besides, miracle remissions aren't unheard of. They're not common, but they have happened."

Ian refused to go down gradually, clinging to less and less life. He contended that he and Caitlin must live fully, whatever time he had. "Trust me," he told Caitlin, with a smile. "I'm a doctor."

"I am too," Caitlin countered, "and I'm not about to be snowed by your justifications and bullshit, Ian. I'm scared too, but I don't know what the best thing to do is." Ian noted the red flush creeping up her neck and tried to deflect her objections.

"We're going to beat the sun to the coast. We're going to fully live every second we have together. Let's start packing."

Part of Caitlin agreed with Ian's live-for-the-moment philosophy.

The next morning, top down, they were on the highway.

Ian drove fast, speeding. "A trooper could rapidly abort this romantic escapist fantasy," Caitlin said, and then, half-kidding, added, "I'll ask him to have you committed. I'll say your judgment is psychotic and you're unable to care for yourself."

Ian grinned, slowed a bit, and tried to change the subject by noting the sun-filled day.

"You're a madman," Caitlin told him, but her all-encompassing smile was coming back. She kissed him, and they sped west.

They drove through rainstorms from thunderheads in Kansas toward the vast mountains of Colorado, via expanses of endless grasslands that nourished herds of mustangs running free. They both teared up at this beauty as they headed for the New Mexico border. The sun was getting ready to set; half of the sky was splashed with broad strokes of gold and magenta, while the other was filled with gathering storm clouds. The mountains reflected layers of purple and gray. They had to add sweaters and roll up the windows to keep the top down.

They held hands like young lovers. He glanced at her gold-brown eyes framed with a background of big sky. "I love these moments with you."

She lit up. *Oh, that smile—it got me from our first meeting.* Instead of toward fear, he wanted the imminence of death to lead to an appreciation of every moment of life.

He glanced again. Her dark, short-cropped hair with highlights of silver came alive in the rushing air and framed her amber-flecked eyes and full lips. She blew him a kiss. It was difficult to talk a lot in the high wind, but he could see her fighting back her knowledge and fear that this wasn't going to last.

It led him to ponder. How do you comfort someone who knows that you are dying and is anticipating your loss? It doesn't help to point out that we are all dying, that life is a fatal proposition. None of us is getting out of here alive. There is no answer to death, other than living right here, right now.

They drove into Santa Fe. Death was nowhere in sight. Their exhaustion did not prevent them from making love before falling into a deep sleep.

Chapter 2

SANTA FE DAYS

They stayed in the Anasazi Hotel for a few days and explored the quaint plaza. They were charmed and impulsively decided to rent a home instead of driving on. They found a perfect place with an exquisite view of the setting sun. The first night there, they watched in amazement. Clouds seemed to ignite in flames as the sun fell below the mountain horizon. They thought the magnificence was over but were stunned at the diamond-studded night sky that followed, expanding to an endless universe. Stars of varying sizes pulsed with a cosmic rhythm. Caitlin and Ian reached out to touch them as they shared the wonder.

They inhaled the beauty of Santa Fe—the sun, the chamisa with its foam-green foliage intermixed with the purples and golds of flowers along the roads. Ian loved the wildflowers, especially the fact that they seemed to grow wherever they wanted, without respect for plot lines or fences. The mountains and rocks—all of nature—seemed to speak to them. The view west to the Jemez Mountains gave them superimposed purple, green-gray layers.

Caitlin thrived in this atmosphere of beautiful art and nature. This gave her the opportunity to break out her Martin® guitar for the blues. She had developed beautiful full tones, reflecting her progress from the voice lessons she was avidly pursuing.

"She's the best teacher I've had in my life," Caitlin would say as she returned from another lesson.

After having taught forensic psychiatry for a number of years, Caitlin had retired and turned back to her interests and talents in the arts. She had spent earlier years of her life touring with a folk dance troupe but, despite Ian's encouragement, had never felt she had the time to reconnect with dance. She read voraciously, worked on sketches, and pursued her music. Ian continued work on a book concerning happiness that he had been trying to find time to pursue over the past decade.

They loved dining at the Road House, a somewhat funky locals' place with great food, where they met a parade of colorful people while at the bar waiting for a table—a farrier, a physicist from Los Alamos, a horse whisperer, an eighty-year-old glider pilot, and a healer who bragged that he could relieve almost any pain by placing his hands on the painful part of the body. As undisclosed physicians, Ian and Caitlin worked to suppress their laughter when he added that he could heal over the phone too, but that his work was "more scientific" if he actually touched his client.

Ian liked to observe that the "shared reality quotient," the amount of overlap in the assumptions of what reality is between individuals, was quite low in Santa Fe. Their favorite description of the local culture was expressed by a sweatshirt logo reading "Carpe Mañana."

Ian and Caitlin walked, absorbed in the magnificent clouds

and the colorful gold, red, and purple sunsets, which they toasted with glasses of full, mellow red wine. "How does it feel to be free in paradise?" Caitlin asked.

"It's a sea change." He smiled.

In Ian's former life, before the death sentence, he had run a psychiatry department, written clinical and research publications, and treated extremely ill, depressed patients who often went into suicidal crises. He'd rarely found time for meditation or work on his happiness manuscript.

All of his work had provided meaning, and he knew of no greater joy than seeing a chronically depressed patient with a life of pain and no capacity for happiness, who had lost all hope, suddenly improve and enjoy life once more. One patient told him, "I had planned suicide, but you seemed so determined that I could get better, despite all the previous failures, that I decided to wait around and try—just to see whether you were deluded or just lying."

Ian had to admit that he had become addicted to seeing this kind of response; being a part of these transformations was like watching the dead come to life again. As a result, he would never give up on the notion that a patient could somehow get better. "If you don't give up on me, I will never give up on you," he would say.

Reflecting on this, he said to Caitlin, "It looks like the clinical practice phase of my life is over."

"If you don't give up on me, I will never give up on you," Caitlin said.

Ian, tearing a bit, said, "touché." He leaned toward her, brushing her lips with his.

At ten the next morning, the doorbell rang. "Bring them right in here," Caitlin heard Ian say.

The men carried fifteen fully blooming phalaenopsis orchids into their Santa Fe living area.

"One for each year of marriage, my child bride. Happy anniversary!" Ian smiled and kissed her as the delivery men scurried about looking for places to put the magnificent plants.

Ian remembered aloud the stir in his department when he started seeing Caitlin, one of his young faculty members and about eighteen years his junior.

"People quieted down when you made an honest woman of me." Caitlin smiled. "Thank you, Ian," she continued with a wave toward the orchids. "These are magnificent. It's been a great journey."

Ian embraced her. "We're very fortunate to have each other," he whispered in her ear. "Where would you like to dine this evening, Mrs. Farrell?"

"Are you asking me out on a date?" She smiled.

"Yes," he said. "But first let's take a drive."

With the top down and the sun warm, they drove through the desert rock with clumps of green piñons and pulled up to a four-way stop sign. Ian was in the passenger seat. As Caitlin pulled forward, Ian noticed a huge sedan approaching at high speed. It wasn't going to stop. He watched, his horror growing, feeling at first helpless, as if trapped in a slow-motion dream.

He burst free, crying out. Caitlin, who couldn't see the racing sedan coming, touched the brake, and the speeding car, horn now blaring, swerved through the stop sign, missing them by inches, and sped away. He was confused, rendered speechless for a few minutes, by the sudden near miss with death that had emerged like a bolt of lightning in the midst of such a peaceful moment.

Caitlin said, "I'm sorry."

"They didn't even see the stop sign; it wasn't your fault."

One of the most beautiful days in my memory, Ian thought

when he finally calmed down, *was seconds and inches from being a bloodbath—a meeting with death.* Life in its fragility was always in the balance, and this time ... it continued. He wondered why.

Chapter 3

THE SHADOW OF DEATH

"I seem to be getting tired faster and breathing harder when we hike," Ian said to Caitlin. "I expected to be getting in better shape." He knew that Caitlin understood that the melanoma metastases were taking their toll. Within a few weeks, he could feel himself in the grip of profound fatigue. Lovemaking was almost impossible. Caitlin didn't complain; she knew what was happening. Ian grudgingly admitted that it was time to head back to Chicago while he could still move.

"It's been wonderful, Ian, but you're right. It's time to go. I think we should fly back. Maybe one of the kids can come out and get the car."

Ian awoke in a hospital bed with Dr. Carlson looking down, surrounded by her oncology fellows. "Oh, Ian, you're awake?

Good!" She smiled. Carlson, at seventy, was spry but could be prickly and tough after years of fighting cancer and seeing her patients succumb after long, losing efforts.

Ian apologized for having blown off Dr. Carlson's previous chemotherapy recommendation and asked what his situation was. Carlson graciously stated that she had heard from Caitlin about their marvelous trip. She looked toward her fellows, who handed her the minicomputer with his laboratory results. "Your lungs are quite compromised, your liver is full of metastases, and your liver function tests are elevated. You have quite a bit in your lumbar spine but nothing in your brain."

Ian moved and felt the lower back pain.

"Why did you bother doing a brain MRI?" he asked. "I only have a couple weeks. I won't be giving any lectures, right?"

He could see that Carlson was pleased at his quick humor. She claimed the test had been ordered because of his "genius."

"That's a nonanswer," Ian replied. He went on to kid Dr. Carlson about failing to practice "economic medicine."

She changed the subject by holding up a half-empty bottle of Grand Cru Classe Bordeaux from his bedside table. "Is this a new chemotherapy that I haven't heard about?" She smiled. The fellows laughed softly.

Ian feigned seriousness. "It's called the resveratrol treatment. As a scholar who has studied the beneficial and life-giving effects of grape skins, I've ordered this potion to boost my health and energy. My associate, Dr. Caitlin Farrell, has been kind enough to obtain this life-giving substance to promote my recovery."

Everybody knew that wine was not allowed in the hospital, and everybody knew that Caitlin had been smuggling it in for him.

"At least put it in the cabinet, along with these beautiful wine glasses, in the event of a site visit from our accrediting body,"

Dr. Carlson said. She asked if he still wanted to accept visitors. Several of his colleagues were asking, but she understood how uncomfortable those visits could be. Doctors found it especially hard to talk to their dying colleagues.

"I'd be more than happy to see anyone who cares enough to come by, with the proviso that they come with a new joke for my pleasure and a contribution to the *Life Is a Joke* volume that I intend to publish, posthumously," Ian replied. He thought, *Speaking of visitors, where is Caitlin?*

Dr. Carlson and her entourage filed out, telling him he had some visitors on the way. Ian wanted to meditate before they showed up. This was not simple for him with the back pain and trouble getting a full breath, but he insisted on meditating at least once a day. He appreciated that the nursing staff respected his meditation time—that if they would come to his bedside to administer medication or some treatment and see him "Zenning," they would return later.

This time, Ian was interrupted before he got started. Two clean-cut men, both over six feet tall and wearing sunglasses, entered his hospital room, asking to speak with him.

"Are you from the IRS? You never give up, do you? Okay, what do I owe?" He laughed at his own joke, a habit that Caitlin frequently commented on.

They didn't smile. "We've arranged for a meeting room and we took the liberty of inviting your wife, Dr. Farrell. We have an important proposition to discuss with you," said the taller of the two agents.

Ian was helped into a wheelchair—he noted a surge of transient dizziness—and wheeled past the nursing station, down the hall, and into a small conference room, with the two men following. Caitlin, looking very perplexed, was seated at a table. Ian had no idea what this meeting was about.

He greeted Caitlin as "babe" and told her he missed her. She smiled and came to him and gave him a lingering kiss on the cheek. They momentarily ignored the two military-looking men, who did not look comfortable with this spontaneous affection.

"Let me introduce myself," said the slightly older agent. Obviously in charge, he took off his sunglasses, put them in his breast pocket, and smiled. "I'm Agent McAlister and this is Agent Simpson. We work for DARPA, whose job it is to develop new ways to effectively assure the security of our country."

Caitlin asked, "DARPA?"

"It stands for the Defense Advanced Research Projects Agency, ma'am."

"What could you guys, involved in secret weapons development, possibly want with us?" Ian glanced, puzzled, at Caitlin, who just looked studiously neutral.

Agent Simpson spoke first. "Dr. Farrell, we have done extensive background checks and have been following your medical problem closely. I'll get right to it. You're probably not going to live more than two weeks. And we don't have much time."

Ian looked at Caitlin.

Ian knew Simpson was right—that his body was riddled with melanoma. He knew it was only a question of what failed first, his liver, his capacity to breathe, or his heart. He admitted only to himself that staying awake had been hard the past few days. He couldn't read much, and his back pain was constant. Caitlin kept him going—that, and maybe his meditation and looking forward to sips of that wonderful Bordeaux.

"We know that your brain is still intact," Simpson ventured.

"Oh, so it was you guys who wanted that MRI done," observed Ian, curiously. "Why? I know you probably have access to unlimited funds, but ... why?" He had refused the neuropsychology battery.

It was a complete waste of time and money, and he didn't have the patience for it.

The agents clearly appreciated Ian's alertness but remained very focused. Agent McAlister answered, "Dr. Farrell, we are here to ask you to volunteer to have your mind transferred to an electronic biochip. We have the technology to do it. Our experience with this project—called Project Phoenix—is that it will end your life, but we believe it may allow your consciousness to be transferred to the chip. We need someone with a scientific background, who can hold up under whatever this new state of consciousness will require. We need a person with intelligence, resilience, and stability. You are a bit too liberal, irreverent, and antiauthority, but ... well ... you handled your plebe year at the Naval Academy without cracking up, and you seem to be able to get along and cooperate with your peers without playing the status games they like to play." McAlister took a breath. He hadn't had eye contact with Ian for the entire speech. "We need your decision in the next two days because you don't have much time. And, of course, we need your brain free of metastases."

Caitlin came to life and stood up defiantly.

Ian stood and embraced her. "Let's hear the whole deal first, Caitlin. It sounds like a grade-C movie plot, doesn't it?" He took Caitlin's hand. He wouldn't mind missing his cancer death, with all the accompanying loss of dignity. He also wouldn't mind making some contribution to science.

Ian laughed. "I know just enough neuroscience to know that DARPA can't be anywhere near making this happen. It's a joke!" Ian felt his energy drain out of him as he looked at Simpson, who answered, "It's no joke."

"When do you need to know?"

"We can only give you two days. After that, we estimate it will be too late."

"Ian, you're not giving this bizarre proposal serious consideration?" Caitlin was both angry and sad at the stark focus on his imminent death.

"Can you leave us alone for a few minutes?" he said to the agents.

As soon as they left, he turned to Caitlin. "Honey, look at me. I love you more than any words can convey. This is who I am! But in a week or so, Ian as you know him will be gone; I'll be a mass of deteriorating cells, maybe metabolizing protein and carbohydrate, gasping for oxygen, still eliminating fluid and solid waste, but it won't be me any longer. I may have a few brain waves, be able to groan, burp, and fart, but it won't be me. Don't fool yourself, Caitlin. I'm being taken away, and nothing can change that." Her hand felt cold in his. "Honey, it can't be helped. But this is my last act. Let me end up, as usual, doing my own crazy thing. Let's at least listen to the whole proposal."

Caitlin was a mixture of independence and sensitivity to loss. She had entrusted herself to Ian and now was about to lose him too. She didn't want to accept Ian's death one second sooner than she must, but she grudgingly listened. They let the two, by this time very uncomfortable, agents back in the conference room.

"Tell us everything," Ian said as Caitlin stared away from the men who were proposing to take her husband's life. When they finished, Ian said, "I have two demands. Should this cockamamie project, by some quirk in the universe, work and I can't stand the consciousness that results, I have to be able to turn myself off. I'm not signing up to be a passive slave forever. And, if this thing works, some mechanism will be in place that will allow Caitlin to be able to communicate with me, if she wishes." He turned to her. "I don't want to hinder you from going on with your life," he said, but she refused to look at him.

The two agents looked at each other. "We can't make those

decisions, sir," said McAlister. "Only Colonel Clausen, the chief of Project Phoenix, could discuss that possibility."

"Now the ball is in your court, gentlemen." Ian smiled.

After the agents left, Ian begged Caitlin to at least explore the proposal with Colonel Clausen. "Caitlin, I'm dying—I have no choice in this. These guys are offering me a choice as to how I die and the possibility of adding to the meaning of life as mine ends. I know you don't want to hear this, babe, but either way, you're going to lose me. Their proposal sounds crazy, but going along may add something useful and at the same time allow me to feel that my death is my choice. Caitlin, making life mean something is what I'm about—you know this."

Caitlin was sobbing, but she nodded. "Okay, Dr. Meaning-in-Life, I know we can't stop it, so do it your way."

He could only hold her. *Death is inevitable, this death that might advance knowledge, on my own terms—this is a rare privilege, given the available options.*

Chapter 4

THE TRANSFER

Ian, who had checked out of the hospital, took a high dose of steroids to be able to attend dinner with Clausen, hoping for enough energy to get though the evening.

At least he felt an increase in strength and certainly appreciated seeing Caitlin in her svelte black dress as they rode to VK, Chicago's hottest dining experience. Everyone wanted to be part of the VK scene, but very few could afford it. Ian took in every bit of the experience; he was fully present.

"You're beautiful tonight," he smiled at Caitlin.

"This is unreal, but I'm going to try to enjoy it," she answered.

"Remember Leonard Cohen. 'You live your life as if it's real'? One of my favorites. Real, unreal, just be here," said Ian, looking at every neighborhood they passed through.

They were helped out of the limo by a very earnest young man. "Probably a Navy Seal," observed Ian.

The restaurant was fashionably dark, with modern, lush decor—modern art and glass sculptures everywhere.

"The colonel is waiting for you," said the young blonde hostess dressed in a clingy, black dress with a very low neckline. She smiled softly and turned to lead them to a private table in the back.

Colonel Clausen, dressed in an elegant, navy-blue jacket with a wine-colored, open-necked shirt, conveyed no hint of the military. The intensity of his blue eyes and his bearing were all that in any way suggested his career as an ace fighter pilot. His missions and daring had filled the pages of several correspondents' articles, and his reputation as a playboy who was as comfortable in the country club set as in locker room high-stakes poker games had been fare for men's magazines. Now in his forties, he was enjoying the rewards of having survived many risky missions. Ian had enjoyed reading about his adventures.

He looks like a fun guy to have a drink with, thought Ian as they exchanged greetings.

Clausen was clearly aware of Caitlin and, in his casual manner, paid her close attention. He waited until they had time to enjoy the fine wine he'd ordered to get down to business.

Ian, despite the high dose of steroids and the very best red wine, had to struggle to eat enough of his exquisite dinner to avoid notice. *Enjoyment is possible, but it takes some effort, when you're moving toward the edge of death*, he thought, though he was proud of the effort he made and experienced what enjoyment he could.

"Well, Ian, I understand that you have some interest in Project Phoenix." Clausen smiled at Caitlin, obviously checking her response. "Here's to the future," he toasted. "Isn't this great Bordeaux? This is the only place in town you can get this bottle. Garçon, could you please bring another? Thank you."

Ian turned to Colonel Clausen. "Your messengers put me under a bit of time pressure, but I did have some conditions."

"Reasonable conditions they are. About the first, we didn't think to design an escape system in the chip." He looked directly into Ian's eyes. "I can only give you my guarantee that we would respond to your request. After all, in that situation, we would have to be able to keep a person comfortable to expect any cooperation."

"I expected that, and you're right. If someone wants out, they're not going to be very responsive." Ian returned Clausen's look, as if to say, *Don't think I would just roll over and do what you want, old boy.* He took a sip of wine. "What about Caitlin? Can you agree to let her be in contact with me?"

He stumbled a bit. "I can commit to being able to make anything happen that will help, Dr. Farrell." He smiled. "Can you be ready to fly to the Phoenix site the day after tomorrow? Obviously you won't have to pack much, but Caitlin may want clothes for a few days."

Caitlin looked very thoughtful but didn't respond. Ian observed how Clausen went straight to the core of the issue.

"You're one hell of a closer, Bill," Ian said, purposely calling Clausen by his first name.

Colonel Clausen smiled. He had pounced with perfect timing. He drawled, "We'll have a very comfortable plane waiting at Midway to take off at five thirty a.m. on Wednesday. My car will pick you up at four thirty." He filled the glasses with that ambrosia and toasted. "Here's to the future, here's to Phoenix, and here's to the both of you."

Ian slowly shook his head, smiled, and thought, *You are a true piece of work, Bill, one slippery dog.* As if in answer to his thoughts, Caitlin just lifted an eyebrow.

The single day they had to prepare sped by. Ian was exhausted after his night out, but he managed to let his kids know he was taking a trip for specialized medical care. He was glad he had not told them of his impending death. Now he could die suddenly of a supposed heart attack. That could happen to anybody, anytime. They wouldn't have to mourn in advance.

He caressed Caitlin's body softly; he wanted to fuse with her, become one as they had so often, but now he was very limited. They fell into a deep sleep, which was interrupted in what seemed seconds by their young driver ringing their doorbell. "I'm here when you're ready, sir."

Ian was in a stupor. Every part of his body ached, his breathing seemed more difficult, and the pain in his lower back was intense. He fought off confusion but had to admit that he was declining rapidly. He noticed that Caitlin was not her usual organized self either. She helped him into the limousine. Ian dozed, despite his efforts to stay awake, on the brief ride to Midway. They drove through a special entrance that led to a small staging area for government flights.

Colonel Clausen, this time in jeans with a gray suede sport coat and soft loafers, was standing in the door hatch at the top of the boarding stairs. "C'mon in! We have a great breakfast and a malt scotch that you have never experienced."

"You plan to get us soused so we won't give you any trouble?" asked Ian.

"No. I just know you appreciate the good things in life." He was ebullient, trying hard to contain his triumphant satisfaction. He smiled at Caitlin. "You're a brave lady."

The plane took off, and Ian fought to stay alert so he could see the Chicago skyline for his last time. All he could say as he gazed out the window and then back to her was, "It makes it all very vivid."

The jet landed smoothly at what appeared to be a deserted airstrip in the midst of the southwest desert. It was anyone's guess what state they were in—Nevada, New Mexico, Arizona, or the California Mohave. All that was visible was a shack-like, single-story building. Its only distinguishing features were some small devices that looked like high-tech cameras, contrasting with the run-down, nondescript exterior that could be seen as one walked up closer. Inside, a shiny, stainless-steel elevator door with a retina scanner next to it was in stark contrast to the primitive building. The young driver, now dressed in camouflage, peered into the scanner and the door silently opened.

"Welcome to the Phoenix All Seasons," said the colonel as he gestured for Ian and Caitlin to board the elevator. It descended what seemed three or four levels and opened. They were greeted by two female officers, in uniform, both brunettes, with big smiles. "Captains Zaposa and Hensley will make sure you're totally comfortable, and after you've had time to rest, I'd love to host you for dinner." Clausen smiled. Though still in casual dress, his demeanor seemed a bit more military than it had before.

The captains took the couple's bags and led them along tubular-shaped halls to a residence area and, finally, into a suite behind large double doors. The spacious living room was windowless but had a feeling of opulence because two of its walls were LED screens projecting views of beachfronts with what looked like a real setting sun above the "horizon." Ian and Caitlin could hear a background sound of soft, steady ocean surf. Huge couches faced the view, and at the back of the room was a bar, discreetly lit. Very soft, cool jazz played in the background. One could even view the "beach" from the posh shower.

Ian and Caitlin showered and fell into a deep sleep, wrapped in each other's arms.

In what seemed seconds later, the soft doorbell rang. Captain Zaposa escorted them to dinner.

Colonel Clausen was in his element, hidden underground in the middle of the southwestern desert. He seemed enlivened with a little more strut in his step, and he bordered on being effusive. He lavished Ian and Caitlin with a dinner you would only expect to see in a castle, while proudly showing off his wine cellar. He showed them his art collection and library. The evening was just short of a gala, only by the absence of other guests and a sextet. Ian was exhausted but, with great effort, barely able to appreciate the fine food and wine. He didn't have much to say and, at times, struggled to remain awake. The project physician, Major Krystal, stopped by and said he would be checking Ian over first thing in the morning.

Clausen turned his attention to Caitlin, who by this time was numb as she fought to comprehend the cognitive dissonance of this "last supper." Ian could see her struggling to maintain her poise in this absurd situation.

Reality was skewed. Clausen was celebrating on the eve of his triumph; Ian was trying to cope with his physical decline and imminent death, and he watched Caitlin fight to retain her social demeanor in a totally surreal situation. It was too late to run. Ian would be "leaving" tomorrow.

That night, Ian overdosed with Cialis with the desperate hope of being able to make love to Caitlin one last time. She hungered for the love and closeness that he created for her. A soft knock awakened them. Captain Hensley would stay with Caitlin, and Captain Zaposa would escort Ian to Dr. Krystal's office, before he went to the transfer laboratory. The captains waited discreetly outside while the two lovers embraced. Ian had experienced enough pain and limitation that, in his meditations, he had reached a state of acceptance of his death. He knew that Caitlin was still struggling and fighting the notion—the pain of separation. "No regrets, my love. We have been very fortunate to have each other and the health to enjoy each other as much as we have."

Caitlin held back tears. "Ian, don't go."

Ian whispered, "Good-bye, Caitlin. Look for me in the great beyond. I'll always love you."

"Ian ... Ian," she murmured, raising her hands to caress his face.

He smiled through his tears and blew her a last kiss as he stepped back, turned, and walked out the double door of their room.

In an effort to keep Caitlin company, Captain Hensley hurried into the suite as Ian left. Ian and Zaposa walked to Dr. Krystal's office, where the project doctor performed a brisk but efficient examination.

"As long as I'm walking and talking, what finding would preclude me from this gig?" Ian asked with a short laugh.

Dr. Krystal's professional demeanor softened. "It's one hell of a situation, Dr. Farrell."

"It's not so hard when you know you're going to die anyway, and that your death won't be pretty." They shook hands and Ian left with a different escort. *It's the damn "last mile,"* he thought as he walked down a long, sterile, tubular hallway.

The emotionless young soldier who appeared to guide him on his last leg of the journey opened the heavy steel door, and they strode into a massive room that was about three stories high. It was full of electronic equipment, and the floor was covered with large, black cables that looked like huge snakes, except for their stillness. At least ten technicians in full space suits with curved, transparent face masks were scurrying about. As Ian was escorted into the room, they all stopped, as if at attention, and the hubbub abruptly became still.

A glass-enclosed observation room was visible along one wall. A door opened and out strode "Wild Bill" Clausen. He sported a shockingly colorful Hawaiian shirt, which contrasted dramatically with the dull tans and blacks of everything else in the room. He almost glowed. He reached out to shake hands with Ian.

A technician brought him some papers and a book that looked like a Bible. Clausen became very serious, which somehow clashed with his shirt. "Ian," he said, "hold up your right hand and repeat after me. I'm commissioning you as a major in the US Air Force." He asked Ian to swear his allegiance to the United States and pronounced him Major Farrell. "You're making history here today, equivalent with our first landing on the moon, Major. Let me express the appreciation of our nation for your sacrifice for your country."

Clausen carefully led Ian across the room, taking his arm as they stepped over the huge cables. They approached a massive, two-story high machine, which emitted a loud humming sound. Out of a large opening in the machine, a sliding table was poised. Clausen helped Ian to push up to a sitting position on the table and then slowly lie down. After a signal from the control room, he said, "Our thanks to you, Major. Anything you would like to say?"

Ian could not get into the solemnity of the situation. He suppressed a smile. "Colonel, this is a win-win for both of us. I get to escape the melanoma feasting on my body, and if things work out, you get to be general."

Clausen blanched, not knowing how to reply.

Ian threw a comic salute, from flat on his back, as he slowly disappeared into the vagina of the machine.

Chapter 5

THE UNEXPECTED

The monster vibrated and roared, sounding as if it were going to explode. This continued for about ten minutes, punctuated by what sounded like a thunderclap, and then it gradually powered down to a faint hum. The technicians ran to extract the platform containing Ian's still body. A technician yelled, "My God, he's still breathing."

Every animal experiment had resulted in the death of the animal, presumed to be secondary to the sheer force of the generated magnetic field that was believed to effect the transfer of the animal's conscious mind to the electronic chip. No one had expected Farrell to be alive after the transfer procedure. In fact, the only advance preparation by Clausen's team was a setup for an autopsy in an anteroom off the main lab housing the huge transfer machine. Since, based on the outcome of animal studies, everyone assumed that the procedure would kill Farrell while hopefully transferring his mind to the specially developed tetra-biochip, the fact that he was found breathing after the transfer procedure was not good news—had something gone wrong?

In the observation booth, Colonel Clausen slammed down his mai tai. "Breathing? What the fuck? Did we fail?" Clausen took a long, deep breath.

"Should I get the crash cart?" the technician bellowed.

Clausen ran out, almost tripping on the cables. "Whoa! Stop! Nobody do anything. Just wait!" He seemed to collapse, frozen in thought. His shirt collar was askew, his head almost bowed. He stared ahead looking confused.

"Sir," a voice came from the speaker on the observation area. "Colonel, the monitor shows a signal from the chip. I thought it was an after-potential, but it's getting stronger—more amperage. I think something transferred!"

Major Krystal summoned nurses to get Ian's limp body on a gurney. Since he was breathing with some effort, they gave him oxygen and took him to their intensive care unit.

In the midst of the chaos, after hearing about the potential measured on the biochip, Colonel Clausen thought, *Maybe it worked after all.* A smile crept across his face, and he regained his composure. "This has been an amazing day. Let's clean up, and then everybody in my conference room at eighteen hundred hours to figure out what happened and where we are."

Lightness. Floating. Is this heaven? Fusion with all, an oceanic sensation—pure aperçu. Nothing. But now in a vibrant, light-filled void. Slowly, it turns dark, black.

No touch, no sound, no smell. A sense of self slowly dawns like a picture emerging from a developing tray. Ecstasy morphs into terror, darkness, isolation. No up, no down, buried alive?

I need to gasp.

I can't breathe. No—I don't need to!

Am I dead? Does consciousness go on after death?

But I can think. How can that be?

A scene from Johnny Got His Gun *flashes—a doughboy in World War I is terrified by confusion and then the roar of artillery. Everything disappears. They tried to let him die, but he wouldn't. He awoke in total blackness with the gradual realization that he had no sight, no hearing, and no feeling—no limbs or face!*

The terror connects to a memory. I am buckled in a crashed plane fuselage, upside down in dark water. Not a sound. Not able to feel the release that had lodged in the button fly of my swabbie pants. I remember madly tearing at my groin to find the lever while holding my breath under water.

There it is.

Releasing it. Swimming up to smash my head on the upside-down fuselage, finding my way around the "wreckage," reaching the surface with a huge gasp, inflating my Mae West. The others waiting for their turn stare at me, looking stunned. Then I see my bleeding fingers staining the water.

I had passed my midshipman dunker drill. Barely.

The awareness of memory is reassuring. I'm me!

I've always feared not being able to breathe. The memory of being trapped underwater still terrifies me—body or no body. The grim humor of the memory of my escape with the release lever caught in my fly eases my terror.

My meditations on my death, weeks ago, come to mind. Thinking of nothing but my own death, the gradual decay of my dead body, and the spirit leaving was scary. At first, I felt trapped as I sought to

walk in the light of death, but after some practice, it was a liberating
experience.

I focus on slow breathing, even if I have no breath.

I can think. What else do I have?

I am conscious.

I remember reading about the vibrant void, a Buddhist concept
of life as a dark void, illuminated by strings of light-emitting jewels,
creating what we think of as reality in their interconnected reflections
of one another.

Where are the vibrant jewels now?

The senior staff assembled around a large conference table. Major
Clausen sat at the head of the table, very much in charge. "Okay,
what's the verdict? What do I tell Senator Samuels from the
oversight committee? And don't start blowing smoke up my ass."
Clausen, dressed in his military casual, with birds on his collar,
sat at the head of the huge table while his staff waited for his
permission to sit. "Captain Borges, with your summa cum laude
in physics from Caltech, what can you tell me?"

The room was permeated with the colonel's intensity, his stern
focus. No one wanted Borges's job at that moment. Borges showed
a facial twitch, but visibly struggled to stay together.

"Sir, we have a definite signal. It resembles the signals resulting
from Dr. MacDonald's animal transfers. It is persistent. We have
no way of knowing what this means yet. Major Farrell's been
taken to the hospital ICU and put on every available type of
monitor. He's still breathing with a heartbeat and EEG activity,
but where is his mind? Is he in his body or on the biochip? The
only test that will give us a clue will be a response from the chip.
We are assuming that, if Major Farrell's mind did transfer, he

would be too confused to respond to our efforts for at least two weeks. Our plan is to start trying contact in a week and, from then on, daily. The CIA has assigned Major Vince Picatta to lead the communication team for dealing with Farrell. He'll start the efforts to contact him through our communication."

Clausen was not satisfied. "You haven't answered my question. What should I tell the senator? Did it work or not?" Clausen was focused like a laser, and his usual easygoing charm had turned hard.

Captain Borges stiffened. "Sir, I would tell the senator that all signs are positive. The increases in firing rates we measured are similar to those in the animals. In two weeks, we will start sending messages through our dedicated system. This will be supervised by Major Picatta."

Colonel Clausen had read Picatta's record. Picatta was just in from the cold after years of undercover duty, which had made Clausen doubtful at first. But then he'd found out what a character this guy was. First, he was a PhD psychologist. Maybe he could keep Farrell from going bonkers, if Farrell was actually on the chip—and conscious. Second, Picatta was gutsy and knew how to get a job done. The story was that he had been sent to visit the Saudis as an expert on substance abuse, but his real assignment had been to take out one of the princes, a terrorist paymaster. The hit was a way to send a message indicating that our intelligence boys knew that our oil money was supporting terrorist attacks against us. He'd pulled off the mission and somehow gotten out with a bottle of fine scotch. *I'll have to keep an eye on this Picatta*, thought Clausen.

"Okay, Borges, I think we're in good shape. Keep me informed and take care of that baby. We can't afford the slightest fuckup. It's like we're back at Trinity for the first A-bomb test. Now let's get a drink. We've earned it."

"What about our Major Farrell on the ground, sir?"

"We don't know if he'll make it. Damn! We didn't expect this. We'll wait and see, of course, giving the major every possible support. We'll watch those potentials on the chip. We could have an intact copy. It just wasn't expected to go this way."

Later, in the officers' bar, Clausen was almost euphoric, making toasts to everyone in the project. He had the same ecstatic feeling as when he had flown a successful mission, flying low "like a bat out of hell" and providing saving cover for overwhelmed troops on the ground. During that mission he had put everything, including his life, on the line and won the cosmic crap game. That was nothing compared to this. *This is really big. This will get me promoted to general. My life's goal is finally within reach.*

Perhaps it was the scotch that put him in a generous mood. He wasn't usually one to share the glory, but he thought he should call Chi and tell her how the transfer had gone. *I can give her some strokes about her invention; make up with her for her demotion before the transfer; and, at the same time, find out if it's possible that Ian's mind could have* copied *on the chip.*

The colonel realized that lateralizing Chi as quickly as they had was a bad move. He took some comfort in the fact that they'd kept her on as a consultant in case problems came up with the technology. Clausen only partly realized how little his technicians knew about the technology Chi had developed.

He found a quiet spot, pulled out his cell phone, and dialed. She answered on the third ring. "Chi, I was going to call you in tomorrow for a meeting, but I don't want to wait. I have really big news. We just did the transfer with Dr. Farrell. We have a signal on the chip comparable to what you reported from animal transfers, but Dr. Farrell lived. At first I thought that his survival meant a failure of the transfer, but with the signals ..." Clausen paused; he thought, *It's just like flying low through the smoke of RPGs and flack.* His tone was unusually diffident, almost apologetic, when he continued, "I'm wondering, Chi—I'm just wondering—is it possible that a copy of his mind transferred?"

"Well, congratulations, Colonel." She was quiet for a few seconds. "I can't explain how Dr. Farrell survived that procedure, but it's entirely possible that a copy transferred. Since the animals all died, we didn't have an opportunity to see what they were like after a transfer procedure. If you have continued potentials from the chip, and particularly if they respond to input, you may have done it. This is totally new territory—working with humans. I'm sure Dr. Farrell is probably unresponsive as yet."

"He has some EEG signals, but he seems to be in a deep coma."

"Colonel, you can't be sure, but it looks like you may have a success."

"Chi, I'm calling to congratulate you personally. You invented the whole process that led to this. If this work weren't top secret, you could be a Nobel laureate."

Clausen remembered reviewing Chi MacDonald's file before he visited her lab to entice her into Project Phoenix. She was the daughter of an African American father, Sam, an ex-Navy SEAL widely known in the intelligence community for his amazing talents for espionage and international assassinations, and a Chinese woman, Meixiu, a PhD in mathematics from Berkeley, who came from a family of scholars who were persecuted during the Cultural Revolution in China. Chi's parents had met in Australia while Sam was on a mission and after Meixiu had fled China. They'd married and raised Chi in Berkeley.

Chi had grown up imitating her mother's Tai Chi workouts as a "dance." When her father would return from his "business trips," the family would spar with one another using Tai Chi and other martial arts. Chi had considered the martial arts sparring as "dancing" with her family, until, when she reached the age of fifteen, her father, adding some wristlocks and kicks to her repertoire, informed her that she now knew martial arts well enough to disable or even kill an attacking enemy. Chi reportedly was amazed at the notion that anyone would ever want to hurt her.

She went on to college and a PhD in neurophysics at Berkeley, where she pursued her fascination with consciousness. She was known to say, "We're all meaningless specks in this multiverse—yet our consciousness allows us to contemplate our past, future, and the almost incomprehensible reality that we are a part of."

"I didn't feel that appreciated when the CIA announced that the directorship of Project Phoenix had been turned over to someone else," she responded.

"Chi, that was not my decision; it came down from above me through the CIA."

"That's very hard for me to believe."

"It's much more complicated than you realize."

"Whatever. I'm handling it."

"Because of the military nature of the application, you have not gotten a fraction of the recognition due you, Chi. What you have accomplished is mind-boggling."

"It's been very exciting. Now I'm ready for some solitude and meditation. In fact, I'm taking some leave to do a Buddhist retreat in Thailand."

"Sure you wouldn't rather meet me in Vegas? We have a lot to celebrate," said Clausen, though he kept the tone light. Five years of effort and he still hasn't gotten her in bed.

He remembered his first meeting with her, how he had been struck by her beauty, as well as her calm distance. She'd seemed totally unimpressed by his position and his interest in her. The research support clearly interested her, but she'd maintained a cool distance that had made him want her even more.

"I'm in it for the research," Chi had smiled as she'd moved her hand to her lap.

Clausen had noticed and sat up straighter. "I'd like to talk you into moving into a new research facility to expand your work," he'd replied, referring to her transfer experiments and particularly her report of persistent signals she had found on the biochip in response to electrical stimulation.

"What do you make of that?" he had asked.

Chi had responded. "I think it's possible to transfer the animal's consciousness, along with its ability to learn, to the biochip."

Clausen had asked her if she were willing to work on a project to transfer a human consciousness. "DARPA needs a human intelligence unencumbered by a frail body for weapons research, Chi," he'd said.

Chi had appeared stunned. "If we ever succeeded in this Frankensteinian experiment, we'd be responsible for a human mind, a soul on a chip. What about that person's feelings and experiences?"

And now, five years later, it had happened.

Chi's first question was, "What support systems do you have in place for Dr. Farrell; has that been considered?"

"I just told you. We don't even have contact with him yet."

"But you might. You need to be prepared."

Clausen bristled at Chi's persistence—her total disregard for his authority.

"We're prepared," said Clausen. He was sorry he'd even called her. "Look, I've got to go." He hung up without even waiting for a response and made his way back to the bar.

The officer's club bar was filled with his staff after their posttransfer meeting. Now it was time to celebrate. Clausen's attention, along with everyone else's, soon shifted to the dramatic tenor voice singing "O Sole Mio" in Italian, by the piano.

"Did we hire opera talent for the officer's club?" Clausen asked.

The conversation quieted, and some applause filled the room. The piano took up "Quando, Quando, Quando," the voice picked up the lyrics in English and Spanish, and the crowd cheered. Then came a rendition of "That Old Black Magic," Sinatra style.

"This guy's taking over the party. Who is he?"

"That, sir, is Major Vince, the Prince, Picatta. He loves to sing at parties."

"Have him in my office at zero nine hundred," Colonel Clausen ordered.

At nine on the dot, Major Vince, the Prince, Picatta knocked on Colonel Clausen's office door.

"Happy to meet you, Picatta. I understand you're with the CIA Behavioral Unit and you've been loaned to us to manage the chip."

"I've been looking forward to meeting you, Colonel. Your aerial exploits are legendary." Major Picatta shook his hand.

"I've heard a bit about you too, Picatta. Is it true about the malt scotch?"

"Not entirely. It was a bottle of Blue Label. The Saudis don't appreciate the malts."

"Too bad. With all that money, they settle for blends. Even Blue Label doesn't come close to the finest malts. Vince, I can see that we'll get along fine, even if I am a bit suspicious that the company sent you to look around Project Phoenix."

"Colonel Clausen, Project Phoenix is the star of the need-to-know crowd. You'll be promoted to general in months, if this transfer works. I'm excited to be part of it." Picatta gestured dramatically, as he talked—hardly like the restraint and distance you'd expect in a spook.

Everything sounds like bullshit, but it's all true, thought Clausen—*really smooth.* "My technical people tell me that it will take a few weeks to confirm that we have a functional transfer. Things didn't go exactly as expected, but I've had missions succeed when unexpected crap occurred throughout my career, and I know you have too."

Vince laughed. "You don't get anywhere taking the easy ones. It's the same excitement you get rolling the dice and winning. And I really love to roll dice."

"Tell me," said Clausen, "why you are insisting that, if we make contact, only you can speak to Farrell?"

Major Picatta became very serious. "I'm a psychologist. If we succeed in contacting Farrell's consciousness, we'll find a being that is starved for human contact and terrified of the aloneness. He's totally isolated, totally sensory deprived. In fact, he may be psychotic from the isolation. This is worse than any kind of seclusion that we could impose on a client for interrogation purposes." He leaned forward for emphasis and lowered his voice to a near whisper, for effect. "He'll be like a guy in the desert with no water. He'll be desperate for any contact. If I'm his only contact, he'll become totally dependent. I'll keep him sane and keep him from being overwhelmed by the terror of his situation."

Clausen smiled. "And he will gladly do anything you ask. He will be fully cooperative, despite his independent character."

Picatta slowly smiled back. "I think we understand each other, Colonel."

Clausen reached in his desk drawer, pulled out a bottle, poured two small crystal glasses, and handed one to Picatta.

Picatta held up his glass. "*Cin cin*," he toasted.

"To Project Phoenix," said Clausen. "I'll enjoy working with you, Major. Please keep me informed."

"Will do. Ciao, General." Picatta saluted with a smile as he slowly strode out of Clausen's office.

A real smart-ass, thought Clausen. *But he seems to know what he's doing.*

Clausen's intercom buzzed. "What is it, Borges?"

"Sir, the electrical potentials are increasing from the chip already. I think we can begin trying to make contact much earlier than expected."

"Call Major Picatta. He's the only one authorized to make contact," Clausen responded firmly.

"Yes, sir!"

Clausen hung up and smiled. *"And away we go!"*

Chapter 6

HANGING IN THE BALANCE

o one at Project Phoenix talked about Dr. Farrell's body, lying in a coma in the hospital suite on the floor above. Caitlin was at his side. He was unresponsive but breathing on his own. The EKG monitor was still bleeping with a regular heart rhythm. The EEG showed mostly very slow waves, but the activity was persistent. It all brought back memories of Caitlin's internship, how she'd loved medicine then. She had been the only intern in her group who'd carefully read over all the procedures; even the ICU nurses had respected her. She'd loved running the codes, while most of her colleagues were happy to just let the nurses take over until the intubation team arrived.

Dr. Krystal was very attentive, but Clausen, who had so earnestly assured Caitlin of his support, was not to be seen. *Colonel Cool Dog didn't plan on this.* She looked down at Ian's body on the hospital bed, noting that he was breathing without assistance. *He probably hopes Ian won't wake up. He doesn't want the inconvenience.*

Caitlin considered that Clausen might see Ian's survival as a sign of failure for Project Phoenix. She wondered if he was hoping that Ian would just die and simplify everything. *The bastard will probably wish that he had ordered his life support stopped when he hears how well Ian is doing.*

She renewed her vow to never leave his side.

Dr. Krystal walked in the room, making his rounds. "Hi, Caitlin, how's Ian today?"

"The same. Maybe breathing more easily, but I don't know why he's still alive."

Krystal studied Ian's chart. He examined Ian, listening to his breath sounds and checking his reflexes. He checked Ian's muscle tone, moving his arms and legs. Then he looked through his ophthalmoscope. "He's in pretty good tone for having been in a coma for this time—reflexes are present and symmetrical. I've never seen anything like this before. It's a great mystery." He looked up at Caitlin. "Could you spare time for dinner with Cathy and me Tuesday night?" he asked.

"Thanks, Paul, but I don't want to be away from Ian in case something happens."

"You've been here for the last three weeks without a break. You have to take care of yourself too."

"You're right. I'm just so upset to see him in this coma, all for the sake of the DARPA war toys. If I could just see one twitch of a response ..."

Krystal stood up from Ian's bedside and held Caitlin by the shoulders, almost shaking her. "Whoa! Caitlin, I understand how difficult it's been watching Ian in a coma, but remember, Ian would be dead if it weren't for DARPA and Project Phoenix. You seem to forget that he was full of metastases and had less than two weeks to live when the transfer occurred. Keep your head on straight about this!"

"Paul, you're right. I'm so desperate to see Ian be whole again that I've lost all perspective."

Remembering the secret meeting he'd attended where the odds of Dr. Farrell's survival were discussed, Krystal thought, *I have to be therapeutically disingenuous with Caitlin. She has to feel desperate.* All he could do was be as supportive as possible.

"Do you think Farrell is going to survive—intact?" Clausen had looked directly into Dr. Krystal's eyes.

"Everything points to his body surviving; there's no way to predict whether he'll have any brain function after the magnetic field he was subjected to during the transfer," Krystal replied.

An agent in a black suit who Krystal had never seen before asked, "Is there a life-support system he's dependent on that could malfunction?"

Krystal was incensed. He leaned forward toward the agent as if he might be going over the table at him, his eyes glaring.

Clausen interrupted, "Dr. Krystal, his survival was unanticipated, as you know. Our liaison from the CIA has raised the possibility that Farrell could compromise the whole project; the CIA is suggesting that it would be better if he didn't survive. They've made the point that, since he may well be demented if he does attain consciousness, it would be more humane if he died in his coma."

Krystal lost it and burst out, "He is not on life support; he's breathing independently. You're too late. Or are you asking for a pillow to accidentally fall on his face? Then perhaps you'll suggest a car accident to take care of his devoted, grieving wife. You CIA guys make me sick!"

He leaned forward and stared at the unnamed agent, who showed absolutely no reaction. "This man was willing to give his life for this country, and now you want to take him out because his survival is inconvenient?"

Clausen intervened. "Dr. Krystal, these guys have to think of the big picture concerning this nation's security."

"Sir, abandoning all morality is not the 'big picture'; people are not military hardware."

Clausen, who had been listening to the argument, paused, looked thoughtfully into space, and then sat up, indicating by his posture that he was taking over. Everyone was quiet, awaiting his response. "I guess we understand Dr. Krystal's position; he's a physician first and a soldier second. We'd all want someone like him to be taking care of us when we need it. He does have a point—this man has offered to participate in an experiment with his own mind, just to help this country with a major scientific and technological development for its security."

The agent looked angry, his cool demeanor failing to hide his true response. "This is a monumental security decision; this guy could be a loose cannon—if he survives."

Krystal, staring down the agent, shot back. "I'll do everything in my power to make that happen."

"Okay, enough!" Clausen broke in, taking over. "That's enough. We're going to let things take their natural course. We owe that to Farrell and his wife." Clausen turned toward Picatta. "If you guys decide to off him later, I can't control that. But nothing is going to happen to him on my watch. Is that understood? The guy is a patriot. He deserves his chance to survive—if he can."

The agent tried to protest.

"That's enough; the decision is made. Captain Borges, will

you please accompany our friend to his Blackhawk. This meeting is over."

Caitlin could see that Dr. Krystal seemed preoccupied as he continued to examine Ian. "Let's see how our patient is doing today."

Krystal finished checking Ian over.

Caitlin was watching. "It seems to me his breathing has eased a lot. Why is that? His lungs were full of feasting melanoma cells. He could only breathe with great effort before and right after the transfer."

"Caitlin, I wanted to talk to you about this, but I didn't want to raise false hopes." He shook his head. "Look. I can't see any metastases in his chest films." They looked at the most recent set of films on the light board. "At first I thought the portable film didn't show it well, but now with his improved breathing, I have to wonder if his cancer is remitting for some reason. Maybe the transfer somehow had an effect."

Caitlin studied the X-rays. "Do you really think the tumors are regressing?" She searched Dr. Krystal's eyes.

"No question about it. They were all over his body before, and now three weeks later, I can't find any on routine films."

"Can you do a more sensitive scan here?" Caitlin asked.

"No, but he's probably doing well enough to airlift him over to MD Anderson. The facility's technology is state-of-the-art— well set up to do sophisticated scans, tumor markers, and check him out neurologically. We'll arrange that. They will be very interested."

Caitlin collapsed into the chair she had barely left for weeks. "Wow," she sighed, "a cure for terminal cancer, and Project

Phoenix is too 'top secret' to let anyone know about it. But Ian may be cured … he may be cured," she whispered.

Dr. Krystal, remembering that meeting, smiled wanly.

Caitlin, as if sensing a decrease in Krystal's upbeat enthusiasm, said, "You don't look as positive as before, Paul."

Krystal responded hesitantly, saying, "We talked about the possibility that Clausen and DARPA might not be too happy about Ian's unexpected recovery. We have to be careful and get you guys out of here as soon as possible." Recovering, he went on. "I do think Ian will make it; we just have to be watchful."

Caitlin looked at Ian, bent over, and kissed him lightly on the lips. "Come back, Ian," she said. "Come home to me."

Chapter 7

OUT IN THE ETHER

*W*here is Caitlin?
Will Clausen contact me or will I be stranded?
Maybe it only half worked and I'm out here, conscious but alone. Is this what death is like? Or will I be reincarnated like the Buddhists believe? Perhaps as a Bodhi tree?

It isn't so bad when I'm in my memory. Actually, it's kind of enjoyable.

Ian slowly learned to focus on cosmic rhythm, his memory of the pulsing stars in the Santa Fe night sky. Instead of breathing, he had learned to use this to achieve a state of no thought for what seemed like a long time, except he had no measure of time. He had always known that his mind provided the best potential to cope with life, but now it was the only thing he had.

He was getting better at hallucinating beautiful memories, to the point where he could start to "see" them in his mind's eye, even without any actual sight. He was also beginning to be able to "hear" sounds and imagine the full-bodied, yet slightly dry taste of magnificent grapes that Clausen had fed him on the eve before his transfer. He wondered if he'd ever be able to taste fine ambrosia again.

Ian was encouraged by what he had accomplished through discipline and through accessing his being-mind functions. He had contained the terror, but he was still very lonely and yearned for Caitlin. Maybe other feelings or sensations would be possible with practice and mental focus. After all, everything is ultimately experienced in the mind. Anything might be possible this way—except really getting Caitlin back.

Back in the massive underground laboratory, Clausen was nervously pacing and looking very irritable, while Major Picatta and his technicians in white pants and long white coats were adjusting dials controlling electrical inputs into a four-foot-long metal tube sprouting wires. Rows of manned computers filled the rest of the high-ceilinged room.

One technician yelled to Picatta, "Major, we're getting a return signal that is increasing as we adjust the frequency."

Clausen, startled, looked up "Have we got some response, Picatta?"

"Just a minute, sir. We're checking for computer inputs; we might have a contact."

What was that?

A tone?

I know I can't hear, but maybe it's an electronic signal.

There it is again.

Damn, almost like my Zen alarm clock that Caitlin used to kid me about—a soft gong. Half the time I slept through it, but it was so much more soothing than being blasted by a buzzer to face the cold, black morning.

Another one. Are they trying to contact me? Maybe they're testing the chip for some response. Maybe I'm not going to be alone. My God, I could live forever if they decide to use a nuclear power source!

What's that?

Sounds like nonsense words, like a cell phone breaking up. But it's not external. I hear it in my mind.

"Major Farrell? This is Vince, Major Picatta, from Project Phoenix. Do you copy?"

How the fuck am I supposed to answer? Do I copy? How?

"Jee-ss-us, he's answering! He said, 'How the fuck am I supposed to answer?' Major, all you have to do is to think an answer to copy!" Vince turned to his assistant. "We have a contact, and he's swearing at me! Holy shit! Open the champagne; just don't spill it on the chip."

Go ahead and spill some; maybe I'll be able to taste it.

"Sorry, Major Farrell. We can't offer you any. Are you okay?"

Call me Ian. It's been pretty quiet here. Not much going on. No parties, no music, not much to see. Can you help me with any of that?

"We'll have to work on that, Major."

Call me Ian, and while you're working on it, please get Caitlin.

"Caitlin?"

My wife, Caitlin. Clausen promised we could communicate if this wild scheme worked.

"Ian, I'll talk with General Clausen."

General? The son of a bitch made it. You tell him congratulations for me, and tell him that I want to talk to Caitlin.

"Ian, the general will be very pleased. I'll talk to him about Caitlin. In the meantime, you may hear beeps as we check the communication system. I'll sign off and be back tomorrow. You're no longer alone, Ian."

Thanks, Major Picatta. I look forward to hearing back.

There could be no tears, but his mind wept. First he'd experienced bliss and then terror and then seemingly endless isolation. He had stayed sane by the discipline of meditation. Ian knew that people generally hated the word *discipline* because, to them, it meant someone telling them what to do, someone else making rules for them. They didn't realize that self-discipline, taking control of your own mind, is the key to freedom. Freedom of the mind—that was everything. He had proven it to himself.

He loved Caitlin and still needed her, even without a body. So what now? All he could think about was "hearing" Caitlin.

I wonder if they can read my thoughts. I have to figure some way that I can have a private thought when they're not communicating with me; otherwise, I'll be their slave. I'll have to work on that.

I can demand to talk with Caitlin, but then what? Could they give me some senses? I have to negotiate.

I wonder how they view me. Do they care that I'm human? Am I human? Do I have a soul, whatever that is? Or am I just a piece of high-tech equipment? Even humans are viewed as expendable by the military mind.

Talk about doing-mind versus being-mind. There's a case in point—the military mind. The military is all left brain—the doing-mind. They can't afford to feel connection with others. Drop the bomb, manipulate the drones to take out the opposition—power with a joystick—and go home for dinner and a movie. The gamelike abstraction of modern warfare makes it even easier, and the weapons increase geometrically in their killing power—wow! What pow-wer!

And our pervasive self-justification—whatever I think, whatever I do is right because it's me.

Here I am, right in the middle of it. How did I get myself into this? By not wanting to die a useless and undignified death? How's that for self-justification? By wanting to make a contribution with my life? Or was it my last chance to feel significant? This speck in the universe wants to feel important on his way out. Significant like pharaohs building pyramids, small-town politicians using their last influence to get a street named after them or, if nothing else works, leaving a dazzling tombstone. Goddamn it. It doesn't matter. There is no lasting recognition. If I'm lucky, a generation or two will remember me. Nice guy, made contributions. Maybe a picture to show to grandkids who would rather chase a chipmunk.

So what is conscious life about? Is it a random evolution?

These are questions that consciousness allows me to ask but not to answer. And when I can't turn my mind off, sometimes I suffer.

And there's no way out.

Ever.

Where is Caitlin?

Chapter 8

LAZARUS

Caitlin found Ian's recovery from the force of the transfer to be painfully slow. Over weeks, she observed spontaneous movements and vocalizations, like someone dreaming. One day while Caitlin was talking to him, he opened his eyes. She saw what looked like recognition in his expression, but she couldn't be sure.

Then one day, his eyes opened and he looked at her and said, "Where am I?"

Caitlin ran to the side of his bed and kissed him and then cradled him closely. He fell back to sleep. She felt like Lazarus's wife, with Ian coming back from the dead.

That was the beginning. Every day, he would wake up, mumble, and then sleep again. No conversation, yet. Caitlin couldn't help but worry that he had been brain damaged by the powerful magnetic field of the transfer procedure. Nobody knew enough to assuage her fears, not even Dr. Krystal. This had never happened before. No human had ever been subjected to this procedure, which involved extremely high-powered magnetic fields, and no experimental animal had survived it. Survival was a complete mystery.

One day, Caitlin, who was dozing in a chair, was awakened by a light pressure on her fingertips. She opened her eyes.

"Caitlin," Ian said, his voice barely more than a whisper. "Caitlin," he repeated.

She collapsed next to him and wept. *He's alive, he's becoming conscious, he recognized me—maybe, just maybe, his mind is still intact. Maybe I will have Ian back from death—as the person I loved.*

Every day after that, Ian's consciousness became clearer and more manifest. Soon he was able to understand Caitlin's explanation that he had survived the transfer and his cancer had regressed, without a trace of metastases. At first he had trouble comprehending, but one day said, "I've been given a new life with you. I'm not going to waste one second of it." He didn't want her out of his sight.

He was very weak, and with urging by Caitlin and the staff, he began physiotherapy and then more strenuous exercise. He slowly became more independent and showed normal sleep-wake cycles. His recovery was gradual, but Caitlin could see continual progress. One day, he actually laughed at his limited function. Caitlin now knew he would become Ian again. They would stroll the tubular halls of their underground quarters, imagining what it would be like to walk in the Santa Fe sun, with the expansive sky and surrounding mountains.

Having spent several months captive in the underground

facility, Caitlin was feeling restricted. Ian saw this and reflected, "When the hell are we going to get out of this place?" He even asked Dr. Krystal to talk with General Clausen who had been conspicuously absent.

One day, two CIA agents entered his room.

"I talked to two guys who looked like you before," Ian joked. "That's what started this adventure." He turned and smiled at Caitlin.

One of the agents spoke affably. "They tell me that you two are getting cabin fever and want to get out of here. We're here to debrief both of you, so you can go back out in the world with a plausible story that will not expose Project Phoenix."

They asked Ian and Caitlin many questions about their recollection of what had happened since they'd come to Project Phoenix. After several visits, the agents returned with a satchel full of documents.

"None of what you remember about coming to Project Phoenix ever happened," said the second agent, who seemed less than affable. "This is what really happened." He gestured toward the satchel.

Ian and Caitlin just looked at him.

"No," the agent continued, "what really happened is written in this history that I'm giving you to memorize. You need to become convincing enough to convey that what happened is what's stated in this narrative."

Caitlin took the file handed to her and scanned it, stopping at certain points, at first looking puzzled—and then smiling at Ian. "So Ian came here, and before any procedures could be done, he suffered a stroke that led to a coma. How does this fit with his hospital records showing that he was dying of malignant melanoma? It doesn't make any sense!" Caitlin asked, looking surprised.

The reply was that it was not her concern what the hospital records stated. These records were already "taken care of."

The couple were asked to repeat back Ian's "new" history in response to conversational questions. No mention of metastatic melanoma. Ian had volunteered for some experiment and had a stroke, resulting in a prolonged coma, but with excellent care and rehabilitation had regained full function.

Several weeks and CIA tutorials later, two more not-so-friendly agents presented themselves. They very sternly told Ian and Caitlin that any leak about Phoenix could undermine the nation's security and could be treasonous.

"We've done nothing but cooperate with everything you have asked," Ian responded angrily. "Don't play your secret spy games with us. Just let us out of this place so we can go on with our lives. We've learned your little script, and your story sounds much saner than what really happened, so we'll have no difficulty in reciting it. I wouldn't want anyone to know that I was crazy enough to agree to this scheme in the first place. I'm grateful it saved my life—by accident, no thanks to you. We'll be circumspect. Now stop threatening us and get us the hell out of this place!"

"Major Farrell, I—"

"I'm not Major Farrell. You're confusing me with the guy you tried to put on the chip. I'm Dr. Ian Farrell."

No response. No change in expression.

The senior agent, quiet until this time, finally responded. "You and Mrs. Farrell are free to go. Captain Zaposa will arrange for you to be flown to wherever you want."

"It's Dr. and Dr. Farrell," Caitlin responded. "And we'd like to be flown to Santa Fe."

"That will be arranged, Dr. Farrell."

Ian toasted Caitlin with his first glass of cabernet in months.

She laughed. "Here we are—they deposited us at Dallas/Fort Worth Airport, we're waiting for our flight to Santa Fe, and you're forced to toast me with mediocre cabernet. It's ironic."

"It sure is. I got into this mess drinking the finest ambrosia that money can buy, when I was dying. Now I have a new life, and I'm drinking bar cabernet. Is there some life lesson in this?"

Caitlin smiled, her eyes again alive with happiness. "There may be some lesson there, but you've already gone off your script. In fact, did the doctor tell you that you could drink wine as part of your recovery from the stroke?"

"Babe, you know that wine is therapeutic for any vascular disease; it's part of my treatment and recovery."

"I've heard that somewhere before." She pecked him on his nose. "C'mon, let's get on our flight to paradise."

The flight was brief, but it felt like the conversations with their "friends" from the CIA had occurred a long time ago. After seeing Ian easily loping down the steps of the deplaning ramp, Caitlin said, "Not bad for a guy who had a severe stroke. That physiotherapy produced quite a recovery."

"Yeah," said Ian. "That part of the story is pretty lame. I guess the CIA didn't have a medical consultant take a look at their narrative. But I doubt most people will do the math." He stopped and reached for her hand. "Look at those mountains, the clouds, the sky—the sun! We're back in paradise," he exclaimed.

In a month, Caitlin and Ian were settled in a home overlooking the Jemez Mountains forming the western horizon, toasting the sunsets—a spot that provided the couple a chance to get reacquainted with life before facing the well-meaning questions from surprised family and friends in Chicago. Caitlin was back at her voice lessons and was catching up with her guitar.

"This time we don't have the grim reaper looking over our shoulder," she observed.

"Life is impermanent for everyone. That's why we should live it fully and not waste an instant," Ian answered, kissing her.

"You don't have to be so Zen all the time, Ian. Stop lecturing; lighten up."

"I don't mean it to sound too serious. Awareness is what makes life so 'now' for me, more than ever, after what we've been through," smiled Ian.

"Well, I'd rather just dance." She turned the blues up, closed her eyes, and started to move, swaying her hips.

Caitlin's sexual interest was more present than in a long while. "I'm not complaining, but you seem much more interested than before," he said.

"I had a lot of time to think about it, watching you in a coma day after day. Let's just say it's my way of making every second count." She stared out over the sunset. The mountains were lit up in the distance. "What are you going to do with your 'new life,'" asked Caitlin, "besides appreciating every second?"

"I want to pick up where I left off on my happiness book and maybe volunteer a few hours at the community clinic. They can always use psychiatric consultations, and many people are in pain. And I'll help you make every second count." Ian smiled and moved toward her.

Chapter 9

LIFE IS CHANGE

"Ian, it's Vince Picatta."

Ian was meditating when Vince called. Practice had led him much deeper, and he was reaching toward Samādhi—a total absence of thought, relaxation of mind, with full alertness.

"You had hardly any electrical activity on the tetra-biochip. We thought something had failed in the system."

It may have been my meditation.

"Yeah, but we were worried. How are you doing, Ian?"

I'm good, Vince. What can you tell me about Caitlin?

"What am I, chopped liver? I thought you'd be happy to hear from me."

There's only one person that I need to hear from, Vince.

"Ouch, that hurt."

Stop dancing around and tell me what's going on.

"Clausen is in Washington, meeting with the Phoenix Oversight Committee. He can't be reached."

I'm not continuing until I get to talk with Caitlin. Signing out.

"Damn, Ian. Clausen and I didn't discuss this. I can't reach him. We have a lot to talk about. We have suggestions for increasing your capacity and an assignment you'll find interesting.

They stared at the blank screen. Had they lost contact? Or was Ian refusing to respond?

"Major Farrell, please respond. C'mon, Ian, don't be a prick."

I let my anger get the best of me. Failed the Buddhist test of letting go, but it got my message across. I've still got my own will, even if I can't turn myself off. At least I don't have to be worried that I'm some programmed robot.

I wonder why they won't bring Caitlin to me. She had certainly cleared their security checks, probably better than I did. I hope she's okay and didn't take my death too hard. She wasn't very happy about my choosing Project Phoenix. I would have died by now from that cancer, but people always hope for some last-minute miracle, and I guess it was a little unusual for me to agree to a procedure that would kill me, almost like suicide. Maybe she's mad and won't talk to me.

No, Caitlin wouldn't do that, even if she's hurt that I checked out and left her. I wonder if Clausen has moved in already. Maybe they're off on a Hawaiian vacation! No, Caitlin wouldn't do that—at least not this soon.

I say soon as if I know how much time has elapsed. No day or night, and no sleep, so I have no idea of time. I'm sure those DARPA guys would want to cash in on their investment as soon as possible, so it couldn't be more than a few months. Or could it? Vince wanted to talk to me about modifications and assignments already.

I guess I'd better get ready to hold out. They think I need their contact. I miss it, but I held on before I knew they were going to be able to contact me. I don't really need them.

"Dr. Farrell? Dr. Farrell? Do you read?"

That damn Vince won't give up. He thinks I'll cave if he gives me an excuse.

"Dr. Farrell, it's not Major Picatta. This is Chi MacDonald. I'm the scientist who developed the transfer procedure. They don't know I'm contacting you."

What the hell? Is this some trick?

"I know it must be hard to understand. I'm the physicist who developed the technology in animals that Project Phoenix used for your transfer. I designed a hidden channel for communication with whomever ended up on this chip. I realized how lonely and terrifying this could be for anyone, and I felt responsible."

How does this communication work?

"It's like a private e-mail circuit, except you receive it like a thought in your mind. Your mental answer appears to the DARPA and CIA agents, or me, like a printed e-mail. I developed this system while developing the quantum mind chip that sustains your mind and memories."

Can those guys read my thoughts? Is everything I think transmitted to them?

"No. They can only see when you respond to their queries. Reading your thoughts is theoretically possible, and I can see why you would worry about it, but in their rush to get this done, the DARPA boys haven't thought of it yet. It would require my input to modify the system at this point."

That's a relief!

"They took over once the design was complete, and I went

from director of Project Phoenix to 'senior consultant' by order of 'General' Clausen."

I know that game since my days in clinical research. The top dog takes the credit. It's an old tradition.

"You might say that, but they don't really know what they're doing. You are seen as a high-tech weapon, not a human being. When I learned that you would be the first transfer, I read all of your writings and everything I could learn about you. The idea of your mind being trapped on this biochip was upsetting. I vowed to stay in touch, if the transfer succeeded. We must not let them realize that I am in touch with you—since I am not military, they don't trust me. But they need my technical input.

"If something goes wrong, they'll call me to figure it out. They don't understand the basic physics of this. They're trying to do more transfers with people they think will be more pliable than you, and it's not working. I have to make these calls short so they don't detect me, but do you have any questions before I leave? I will get back to you."

Chi, can you tell me why I can't talk with my wife, Caitlin?

A long pause followed.

Did something happen to Caitlin?

"No, not Caitlin."

My God, please tell me. What's going on?

"I don't know quite how to say this. Do you remember that the transfer process killed all of my experimental animals when we first demonstrated the effect?"

Yes. I knew that, and I accepted it.

"That's why no one, after the transfer, was ready to find the man we're now calling Ian-1, in a coma, breathing, with a heart rate and active EEG. Ian-1 spent two months like that, before showing some signs of response. Caitlin slept by his bedside and was in the recovery room in the DARPA hospital twenty-four hours a day. She didn't lose you, Ian."

But what about the melanoma? I was barely getting enough breath. My lungs were full of tumor cells and fluid.

"It appeared from the scans and Ian-1's improved respiration that the cancer was shrinking. In fact, Dr. Krystal couldn't find evidence of the metastases in his scans at all. It looks like the transfer process, with the intense magnetic field it generated, cured Ian-1's terminal cancer."

She paused. "When Dr. Farrell woke up, he recovered his mental function even though the transfer procedure had made a complete copy of his mind."

Which is me.

I'm a copy?

Ian lives, and Caitlin has lost nobody. She still has her beloved Ian. She came close but didn't lose anything.

Does she know about me, the copy, Chi?

"No, that's classified at the moment. The reason they can't produce her for you is that she doesn't know you exist, and they don't want her to know. At first, when Ian didn't die, they weren't sure what had happened. In the meantime, Caitlin nursed Ian back to life. In parallel time, the DARPA boys have contacted you. Clausen would have preferred that Ian had died as planned, but now he has to deal with Ian-1 and Ian-2, which, by the way, is what we're all calling you."

I can't comprehend this.

Ian still lives. No wonder Caitlin didn't fight to contact me. She doesn't know I exist. And she has Ian.

I am not Ian anymore.

Caitlin has continued to love Ian as I have continued to love her. The full impact of this blunt truth hit him. The realization that he was a copy of the original Ian, instead of being "Ian"—the only Ian—was the horrible truth that slowly filled his mind.

I'm a copy? Is that what I am? A copy?

He paused, the thought becoming real, unavoidable.

I'm not me—I'm nothing.

I feel empty, transparent. I don't exist …

Chi, help me. What am I?

"Maybe I shouldn't have told you, Dr. Farrell. I feel so sad."

After a very long period of no response, he replied simply, *Chi, I'm thankful I heard it from you.*

"Don't let on that you know about this to Major Picatta, Ian. We have to keep our contact secret."

Again, no response came immediately, and then, *Chi, can you leave me alone now?*

"Of course, Ian. I want to help with your pain, but I know you need some time for this. Bye, Ian-2."

I feel totally empty and totally alone.

Then it hit him—*was I really I before this? Did I exist as an individual?*

He remembered the Buddhist notion that nothing existed independently but only in relation to multiple interrelated causes—by itself, anything is empty. Nothing exists alone; the concept of "I" is an illusion.

The notion of inter-being—so I was never I. Without my parents, their parents, our sustenance by the planet, the sun, the clouds and their recycling of water, my teachers and friends, there is no I. Now, what am I? I am an inter-being. Am I less than I was before the transfer? My consciousness is me—I inter-exist!

But I'm alone.

I'm all alone in the void.

No Caitlin. But, I exist—very much alone.

Still, I feel like a person—somebody—again. Inter-being.

Then inter-being became personal. He realized, *There is only one human being in this universe who cares anything about me— Chi* ...

Chapter 10

CHI'S DEAL WITH THE DEVIL

For the past year, Chi MacDonald had been totally immersed in her attempt to transfer signals of consciousness from vervets to a quantum biochip she had constructed with its billions of microtubules. She was in her lab day and night, to the point that her technical staff began to worry about her. She was in the lab when they left and again in the morning when they arrived. She shrugged off their concerns; this was her journey of discovery, and nothing was going to stop it. Her experiments progressed rapidly. She began measuring signals from the chip after transfer procedures involving the use of a magnetic field generator.

One day, an attractive senior air force officer and a briefcase-carrying aide wearing sunglasses strode into her lab. "Dr. MacDonald, I'm Colonel Bill Clausen, director of Project Phoenix."

"Welcome to my—"

"I never realized that scientists could be so beautiful. How can they keep you so isolated here?"

"Well, I'd rather be at a university, but DARPA will fund my work no matter what I need here, and my work is exciting."

"I'd love the chance to expand your source of excitement." Clausen smiled. "But we came because your work has been so successful. We'd like to talk you into moving to a new research facility to expand it."

"Oh, you want to expand my excitement and my work?" Chi smiled. "Are you hitting on me?"

Clausen looked taken aback but recovered his jovial, smooth manner. "You're quick! Have you ever heard of Project Phoenix?"

"No."

"Well, it's top secret, but if you come aboard, we'll get anything you want."

"Anything I want for what?"

"Let me take you to dinner and we'll discuss it."

Colonel Bill Clausen, dressed in a burgundy, open-necked shirt; navy-blue sport coat; and gray loafers, met her at the door of Vivace and ushered her in. Their table was waiting.

"We're aware that you repeated that rat experiment in primates and found a signal that lasts on the biochip."

"Yes, the signal that I measured from the vervets' brain persists on the chip after the magnetic transfer. It takes a massively powerful magnetic field. It looks like the consciousness signal is transferring to the chip, but the vervets die. I wish I could interpret the chip's sustained wave activity. The signal was the same as the vervets' brains showed when conscious and alert."

"What do you think is going on?"

Based on Clausen's expressions and body language, it was difficult for Chi to decide what he was up to. *Does he want me to work on his project, hook up with me, or both?* she wondered. "If you order me a martini, no ice, with a lemon twist, I'll tell you." Chi smiled softly.

Clausen immediately ordered and apologized for his "scientific intensity."

They changed the subject to the weather, until the martinis arrived and Chi took an appreciative sip, while Clausen watched.

"Well, it's hard to prove, but there is some indication from evoked potentials that the chip has the vervets' conscious awareness and capacity to learn."

"Why did you pick vervets? I hear they're very expensive."

"Everything is expensive if you do it right. Vervets are advanced; they are very social and have a different cry for different situations—a proto-language. I wanted an animal with certain similarities to a human intelligence and consciousness."

"How could consciousness be transferred to a biochip?" Clausen asked as he ordered another round of martinis.

"Based on quantum mind theory, it would be theoretically possible to transfer an animal's consciousness, along with its capacity to learn, to the chip. We constructed it with a network of microtubules like those hypothesized to exist in neural nets in the brain. With enough power—and I used all the juice I could muster—I almost blew the magnetic inducing coil. I can't prove it yet, but it's a possibility. See why I get enough excitement here in this isolated spot? It's electrifying! Pun intended."

Chi could see that Clausen was struggling to maintain his focus on the science of their discussion. "I know of your background, including your father and the martial arts," Clausen blurted out. "Stories of your many talents have preceded you." He smiled.

She smiled, accepting the martini he offered her without hesitation. "I thought I was known for running up the largest electric bill ever," she said.

"No, I was referring to your ability to disable Marines in heat," he replied. "The word about you is out—don't try to fuck around with Chi. She will kill you with a chop while giving you a smile."

Clausen had caught Chi by surprise. He was referring to the time she'd disabled a former Marine technician who'd tried to pin her up against a wall in the lab. Chi had flipped him on the deck and stopped her knife hand a small distance from his throat—a potentially lethal blow.

Chi recovered from the initial surprise and responded calmly. "Oh, you mean the one who wanted to dance? Yes, we had a dance together. We reached a full understanding."

Her unruffled retort neutralized his verbal parry. She looked him straight in the eyes, smiled, and casually sipped the martini.

Clausen, looking a bit shaken, continued, "Dr. MacDonald" (*what a strange name for this oriental beauty*), "I'm the director of Project Phoenix that has been funding your research. We have followed your recent studies and would like to talk with you about expanding your work. We'd like to use your technique to transfer a human."

Chi looked taken aback. "Could you repeat that? Why would you think I could or would do something like that? Even if I would agree to the ethics of what you're proposing, I'm years away from even considering something like that."

He had finally gotten to her. "Why would you even consider such an attempt?" she pressed.

"DARPA needs a human intelligence without attachment to a frail body. You're aware that the human brain can perform certain tasks much better than our highest capacity computers. What we want to develop is a chip with the pattern recognition and imagination of the brain."

"What about the soul of that human brain?"

Clearly, Clausen had never thought about that.

Chi's calm demeanor shifted; she stiffened. "We're not talking about a piece of electronic hardware. With a human mind comes a consciousness with feelings and values, not a robot. How will you separate the brain function from human consciousness, Colonel Clausen?" Chi asked in a very serious tone. "If you ever succeed in this Nazi experiment, you will be responsible for a human mind. What about that person's feelings?"

Clausen realized that she was really tough in her scruples. "Dr. MacDonald"—he smiled, holding back his annoyance—"it's exactly your knowledge and your concerns that we need to pursue this goal."

Chi felt confused. She didn't trust Clausen for a second. He was proposing a far-out project without a trace of awareness of the implications. "What do you want from me?"

"Tell me what you need to work on this. The support we can provide is unlimited. We're talking about a modern day Manhattan Project. I will manage it; all you have to do is tell me what you need—how many assistants, what equipment. I'll take care of funding. I want you to be able to focus on this one goal. By the way, this is top secret. From the time you begin, you will be assigned a security detail when you travel to meetings, which I know that you often do," he went on, intensely observing her reaction.

I think I just lost my appetite. This guy controls the means to support such a venture, Chi thought, suppressing an instinct to get up and run out of the posh restaurant. "I doubt you can make enough electric power available to even approach this project."

"Is that a limiting factor?"

"Very much so."

"Then we'll hire some people to help you estimate the specifications for the equipment you need to generate the field. We'll bring in new power lines from the nuclear plant that's only about a hundred kilometers away from the underground laboratory we're building. By the way, did you notice the construction going on at the desert site that houses your lab? That's so you can expand your floor space for whatever people and equipment you'll need."

"I wouldn't need many people, only a few really good technicians and my former research partner, Dr. Chen, if he could be talked into moving from Berkeley. That would be a good start, if it's possible. I have to think about this."

"I know you want to consult with your dad, but he's outside of the country right now, so you won't be able to reach him."

She was stunned at the invasiveness into her personal life. "Did you plan it that way, Colonel?"

He smiled. "How about another hypnotic martini? I didn't know that people of your generation appreciated them."

"As you apparently know, I'm very close to my father, and he has taught me to appreciate a wide range of things, including a good martini." She gazed directly at him. "I don't know how he would feel about the intelligence you have obviously collected regarding me, but I'm interested to see what he knows about you, Colonel."

Clausen looked visibly shaken. The last person he wanted after his ass was Sam MacDonald, the "Sweet Assassin." He mustered a weak smile. "Well, I don't mean to be pushy. It's just that we need you to do this, and we're willing to put whatever assets necessary into it. I hope you'll decide to take this opportunity to help your country."

Chi held back a sarcastic laugh. "The last refuge of a true scoundrel is patriotism, Colonel."

He recoiled but gathered himself, smiling. "You will be a challenge to work with. May I call you Chi?"

"Sure. And may I call you Wild Bill?" It was the nickname he had earned in his colorful career as a jet pilot.

He appeared clearly surprised at her knowledge of his past but recovered, saying, "Just Bill would be fine, Chi."

"If you wish," she replied.

"Get back to me next week?" He smiled.

"Do you have a contact, or should I just express my agreement out loud in my apartment, knowing you will hear it? Can you discern people's thoughts with your surveillance equipment?"

Clausen smiled and held up his glass. "Not yet, but we're working on enhanced surveillance techniques. Here's to next week."

"I'll call you," she said, rising to her feet. "Guess I'd better get some sleep."

"I'll have them bring that sleek Porche Carrerra® around." The colonel nodded to one of his watchful staff on their periphery, who went to call for her roadster.

"I'll be in touch," Chi said.

Clausen smiled. As he watched her walk away, he added, sotto voce, "I'd love to get to touch that hot body of yours."

Chi thought long and hard about Project Phoenix. She tried to reach Sam but couldn't and discussed it with Meixiu, who, as usual, was cautious.

Two years later, Clausen's phone beeped, indicating a call from the lab.

"We've been able to transfer the consciousness signal from a vervet to our latest version of a tetra-biochip," Chi announced. "The signals from the chip have continued, and we think it's capable of learning and responding electrically, putting out evoked potentials in response to inputs."

"What the hell does that mean, Chi?"

"We think the entity on the advanced biochip can respond and even learn. We can't be sure, but it appears that we've transferred some form of consciousness from the vervet. Would you like to come over and see if we can transfer your mind?"

"Damn it, Chi, that's not funny. For three hundred million dollars, you have a chip that gives off a signal and what you call evoked potentials."

"We've gone as far as we can in animal models, Bill. The next step is to build a higher capacity tetra-biochip and increase our magnet sizes. We'll need more power. The new biochip will take about a year if we're lucky." Chi smiled.

"How about tennis and dinner this Friday?"

Chi was superior to Clausen and ran him around the court. All he could do was hit his monster serve by her occasionally. He seemed happy just to watch her graceful body as she took one game after the other from him.

"Okay."

"See you at the club about three."

Clausen put his feet up on his desk for a few seconds and then reached for the phone. "We'll be ready for a human in about a year. It's time to start developing a list of potential subjects. We need a successful scientist, emotionally stable, able to cooperate, who has a terminal illness that doesn't compromise his brain and who will likely die in within a year." Clausen tapped his fingers on his desktop, annoyed with his consultant's concern about the timing of the terminal illness. "Why do you think we pay top medical consultants?"

He listened and then shot back, "Nobody needs to know why we need this guy." He picked up his putter and placed a golf ball on his small, artificial putting green. "Okay, it could be a woman, but I'd rather deal with a guy. Don't make any excuses; this is top priority. Do you realize that we're going to make Phoenix a huge success in another year?" He lined up the putter. "You're damn right. Now get busy, and I'll give you six strokes next week. I'll send the specs for the subject. Ciao, buddy. See you at the course."

Clausen had gotten nowhere near his personal goal with Chi, but she'd produced for him beyond expectations in the laboratory. By the time new power lines were brought in from the nuclear power facility, Chi had created a larger, more complex chip after producing a crystalline material saturated with billions of microtubules. Next, with her input, a team of physicists at Livermore labs had produced a very high-powered magnetic field generator.

Several months later, Chi called Clausen excitedly. "Bill, the tests of the new high-capacity chip suggest that it has the ability to perform as a quantum mind alternate. The power is there now, and the initial tests of the new quantum field generator look good. We've successfully completed transfers from three vervets, and all three show persistent activity on the chip. The density of the field kills the vervets, but the signals persist and respond to stimuli."

"Whoa! Hold on, sweetheart. Slow down. Just tell me what this means."

"It means that, in three months, we'll be ready to try the first human mind transfer."

"Holy shit. Why didn't you say so? That's great! I was beginning to wonder how long you were going to take, but as usual, you caught me by surprise. How about a celebration dinner?"

"Not so fast. I said we'd be ready for tests in three months. That doesn't mean you have your desired product, whatever you expect to do with it. We have to have some discussions about just what you are going to do if you get a successful human transfer."

Clausen dropped his casual, almost seductive tone. He became Colonel Clausen, commander of Project Phoenix, his voice changing to that of the officer in command, ordering his underlings. "Dr. MacDonald, let me remind you that you are an employee of Project Phoenix, which has invested millions in you, under my direction. Your contract is to work on the development of a system that will provide the capability for a human mind transfer. What that transfer, if accomplished, will be used for is not your concern, and you do not have authority to make any decisions regarding the use of your work product. Do you understand?"

"Yes, sir!"

"Sorry, Chi, but just focus on getting to the point we can do a transfer, okay?"

"Yes, sir. I need to get back to work, okay?" Chi responded with a military tone.

"Sure, we'll talk later."

Colonel Clausen smiled. He could taste his promotion to general. He made a call. "Have you guys found a prospect yet? I just learned that we'll be ready for our first subject in three months. Don't hold this thing up now, okay. Call me as soon as you can get me his dossier. I want to look it over. Roger.

"What?" Clausen couldn't believe what he was hearing. A call from Senator Samuel's office was something to consider. "Who is Buzz Stevenson?" he demanded. He did not care if the man had prostate cancer. As he listened further, his concerns grew. The connection to the Cosmic Quest Church was not good. "All we need is a celebrity for our first try. This guy is worth gazillions and probably thinks he can become a god this way. Tell them we're not ready yet—that it may be a year or two. We need a realistic prospect. Get on it."

Now he had to set up a technical command structure to take over the direction of the project. He knew he had to get rid of an uppity, bleeding heart. Besides, he didn't want to blur the question of who had accomplished this masterpiece. He knew that no one else understood the fundamentals, and he had to keep Dr. MacDonald around as a senior consultant in case they ran into some glitches.

Chi had felt anger when Clausen had turned on her. But then she'd asked herself, *Why are you surprised when the devil demands his due?*

She had known the guy was a snake, despite his charm, and now, she shouldn't be surprised that he was taking back all control as the transfer succeeded. She assumed that he wouldn't be dumb enough to fire her. She thought he was intelligent enough to know that nobody else really understood the intricacies of Project Phoenix, despite the people he embedded in the lab. She realized she might be relegated to a consultant role without authority. *You could refuse,* she told herself, *but as long as he needs you, you might be able to help the poor soul who ends up on this chip.*

It was a new game.

Chapter 11

SUNYATA

Sunyata was more self-preoccupied lately. Chi's contact surprised him and pleased him at the same time.

"Dr. Farrell?"

Chi.

"Can we talk, Dr. Farrell?"

Chi, have you heard of Sunyata? Almost no one has.

"Yes, I have read and reread *Sunyata*, Dr. Farrell. It's the prize of my collection. What makes you ask?"

Full, solid emptiness—that is Sunyata. Do you think that description could apply to an electronic abstraction like me?

"You're thinking about losing Caitlin. I'm sorry you're suffering."

I'm nothing. I thought I was lonely before, but I always had the hope that I could be with Caitlin again, even if it was only a conversation. I keep remembering Nietzsche's quote on marriage— "Most of the time you are together will be devoted to conversation." Now I don't even have that, and I'm lost.

"I understand how you feel, Ian, I would feel that too."

You know, Chi, I can see why Clausen couldn't be honest. DARPA makes secret weapons. To them, I'm a high-tech weapon. They haven't told me what they want to use me for, but they didn't create me in a spirit of charity, and they can't afford to take chances. They have to protect their investment. Ian-1's fortunate that they didn't kill him. He's a complication, you know.

"That's very true. He is. But I'm concerned about you."

Sunyata was struggling with a strange mix of feelings and sensations. He felt an emptiness as he contemplated the reality of being nothing but a mind copy of Ian Farrell. But at the same time, he felt twinges of desire for Chi, who was expressing her concern for him. He wondered to himself, *How can I feel empty and sexually turned on at the same time? How can I feel that tingling in my penis as it begins to become engorged with blood, as I become aroused, when I'm just a cloud of electrons with no body?* He remembered that the brain is capable of producing "phantom limbs" in amputees. Was consciousness alone enough for desire?

Thank you, Sunyata responded, *but I don't know what "me" is. From now on, though, I know this—Caitlin is connected with Ian, who I used to be. I am a copy. She doesn't know I exist. If or when she does learn about me, I will be an abstract curiosity. My Ian-ness will not mean anything to her. Her Ian is alive and with her. I am an electronic freak.*

"I don't feel that way, and I don't think Caitlin would either. I hope you get the chance to find out."

I can't wait for that, Chi. It's driving me over the edge, except there isn't any edge.

"I'm afraid I'm the one who created this scenario, Ian."

I'm not Ian anymore, Chi. I can't take being Ian. I've thought about it, and I'm changing my name to Sunyata. Full, solid emptiness. That's me. Do you understand why?

"Yes, Sunyata. I'm deeply sorry for your pain, but I admire the way you're dealing with it."

Nothing is more important than being understood, Chi. Thank you. I don't know where you came from, but you've helped a great deal. Please know that. Now I need to be alone for a while.

"I understand. Good-bye, Sunyata."

Let me out of here! There's no way out. I'm screaming! Yet, like the tree falling in the forest, no one can hear me. With no one to hear, do I exist? Talk about impotence, try nothingness. How can I feel when I'm nothing?

But isn't this what my namesake, Sunyata, actually pursued—full, solid emptiness, through silence?

Sunyata said to his followers, "I have nothing to teach, nothing to sell," and sat, silent. And he had a body, an identity, which he disavowed. His followers adored him and were happy just to sit by him in silence. They felt inspiration through that experience.

I have no physical presence like he did. The only one who sees me as a person is Chi, and all I know about her is that she developed the chip that created me and she seems very compassionate.

She is the only person I have ever met who has read Sunyata.

She certainly seems understanding. I wonder how old she is. She's accomplished a great deal. But her pattern of communication makes me feel she is fairly young.

Sunyata enjoyed thinking about Chi MacDonald—wondering about her and what might she look like. He tried to visualize her in his mind's eye; at first all he could conjure were visions of Caitlin. This was bittersweet and disturbing. How could he be enjoying anything? He was nothing, yet he felt desire and enjoyment. How could this be? His thoughts and feelings seemed mixed up—contradictory. Painful pleasure ...

I have to let go of Caitlin; I must let go.

He forced himself to try to imagine Chi as a woman; it almost became a game. After all, he had little to base his fantasies on. She was a brilliant, compassionate, and clearly independent woman—in that sense, just like Caitlin. But the differences between the two women were clear. Chi was a physicist, clearly into technology, and she had to have devoted herself to research in order to have developed this prison that held his consciousness. Her concern for him conveyed a sense of guilt for what she had discovered. Sunyata could remember his own preoccupation with his clinical research when he was Ian. Caitlin would kiddingly call him a "research junkie." Maybe he shared that with Chi.

He could visualize her tight body, naked, with dark, olive skin; full-nippled breasts, and a taut abdomen with a small patch of black pubic hair. She smiled at him, looking very comfortable. He wanted to touch her—*oh, if only I could!* He felt fullness and desire in his loins, except he had no body. He noted that it was pleasurable playing this game. It made him feel like he had a body after all.

Am I just blocking out thoughts of Caitlin? Or am I developing a dependency on the only human I have in my new life who has any concern for me?

How could he be having these thoughts and sensations? He didn't really know Chi as a person. Was this pure loneliness—grasping, desiring? Was her interest and concern real? It was either nothingness or Chi's concern—and these confusing feelings.

Sunyata remembered seeing patients in his former self's psychiatric practice—listening to countless stories of love, lust, and dependency from his patients. He recalled trying to help them sort through their relationships. Was it really love or was it lust driven by evolution—the force to reproduce—that made us feel sexual attraction? Sometimes a person was driven by a need to be taken care of, to attain a feeling of being loved that never seemed enough. The person cloaked this need in adult sexuality, when it was really the missing sense of parental love that he or she was seeking. This led to disastrous relationships.

Am I getting hooked on the only person who seems to care for me? Sunyata considered.

He gave way to the stirrings of sexual desire—the feelings he'd had in his loins as a young man, when he would run five blocks to be with his beloved girlfriend, hold her, sneak away, and love her. How could this be? Where did those desires really exist? It felt as if they came from his genitals, but they were really perceived in the mind. *That's it*, he thought. *We only need our bodies to procreate with evolution's call—that and to nourish and support our mind. And eventually, our bodies give out and we die.*

I thought evolution was through with me, but then evolution was through with me before the melanoma took over my life, and I still had sexual desire for Caitlin. I'm certainly not letting go of desire, but this feels good, as preposterous as it seems. What can it hurt? Why shouldn't I enjoy all the benefits of consciousness that I can? Can I let myself do this and still be Sunyata?

Chapter 12

BACK IN SANTA FE

I t was one of the few cloudy days in Santa Fe. A front was
moving in from the west, delineated by the mountains. The
piñon trees outside the large windows were tossing their
branches in the gusting wind. Caitlin was reading. She looked
up and saw Ian at his computer, deep in thought.

"Ian, you seem more preoccupied the last day or so. Is anything
bothering you?"

"I keep going over my waking up, as if from the dead. I feel
different, Caitlin. I keep asking myself, why am I still alive? What
am I meant to do with my 'extra life'?"

"Ian, you asked yourself that question way before the transfer."

"It's a stronger awareness now. Gradually coming out of my
coma with you emerging out of my blurry confusion is repeating
in my mind."

"Maybe it means it's time to give me a kiss!" she said.

Ian walked to her, bent over, and kissed her as she snuggled into the couch with her book. He hesitated and gazed at her face. "We are so fortunate," he said, "but I keep wondering what I'm meant to be doing. Is it enough to be doing clinical work and teaching, or should I be doing more?"

"You've always tried to cram more into whatever time you had."

"There's something else, Caitlin. I keep having the feeling that my thoughts have an echo."

Caitlin put down her book and looked pensive. "What do you mean by *echo*?"

"I'm not sure," Ian responded. "It's like something present in my mind that I know can't be real but at the same time, it is real, or at least it feels real."

"I'm not sure if it's anything like what I felt when Dr. Krystal told me you didn't die during the transfer; their voices echoed in my mind. I was so grief stricken. It was as if I were floating above the conversation watching them tell me. And then came the days of hoping, watching for any slight change. I was afraid to leave the room, afraid that everything would stop while I was gone. Nothing felt quite real, like shadows and echoes. It seemed that, somehow, my life force and love was keeping you alive. Is what you're feeling anything like that?"

Caitlin was intense, but she was smiling at the same time. Ian pulled her up and embraced her. "Your life force and love probably did keep me alive. They still do." They kissed again. Ian was consumed in the moment.

But a moment later, when they'd broken apart, he said, "Caitlin, what you described sounds sort of similar, but I keep hearing actual echoes of my thoughts about all the pain in the world. It's like a voice, like my voice, that is repeating many of these thoughts, and I keep feeling I'm not doing enough to address it. I know that sounds grandiose. I just keep thinking that, over and over, and it's as if I'm thinking it twice, or someone else is thinking it at the same time. What should I do?"

Caitlin hesitated. "We don't know the answer," she said.

"But have you noticed any changes in me? Am I the same since the transfer as I was before? It's hard to be in the moment when my thoughts echo like that."

"You've always struggled to be in the moment, but you're more preoccupied. Otherwise, you seem the same. And this echo; you've never mentioned that before."

"I'm pretty old to be developing schizophrenia, but it feels like somebody else is thinking my thoughts. Of course, who knows what that blast of magnetic fields did to my brain?"

Caitlin was quiet for a few seconds, and then, hesitantly, she said, "You know, Ian, we never really heard any more about the transfer. We assumed it didn't work because you survived, but the DARPA boys never said anything. Of course, who'd believe anything they told us anyway? Is it possible that some aspect of your mind did transfer? Could that account for the echo?"

"Sounds far-fetched, but you're right. They never really said that the transfer failed. They just let us come to that conclusion ourselves. In fact, they stopped talking about the transfer. Neither Clausen nor anyone at Project Phoenix expressed any concern or much less made any comment about my recovery. Not a word."

"When you were in the coma, I got the impression that everyone in that group was hoping you would just die, except for Dr. Krystal. In fact, he appeared to be fighting to get you the best of care."

"I wonder if anything about the transfer technique or theory was ever published. It was developed in some animal model first. Clausen told us that. Maybe before DARPA put me through the transfer, some basic research on the procedure was published. I'm going to see what I can find."

A few days later, Ian carried a printout into the living room, where Caitlin was practicing her guitar. "Caitlin, this is really strange! I found one publication about five years ago by a Dr. Chi MacDonald from Berkeley. Look, I found and downloaded the article through PubMed. Ian held up the reprint. "It's amazing. Dr. MacDonald found evidence of lasting activity on a biochip she had designed. After the procedure, the signal she detected appeared as a persistent response to electrical inputs suggesting something actually transferred. All of her animals died. What's really strange is that, after a finding that startling, not a single follow-up study is available. That would almost never happen, unless MacDonald couldn't replicate the finding or made up the original data and was exposed."

"Or …" Caitlin began.

"Or what?" Ian asked.

"Or the government suppressed the publication of further research," she finished.

He smiled broadly. "D'ya think? We know something about information being suppressed, right? And why was Clausen promoted to general right after the transfer attempt?" He sat down next to her, and they reached for each other.

"What are you going to do, Ian? What's your next step?"

"I'm going to try to find Dr. MacDonald. I've already Googled her, and I can't find a single reference to Dr. Chi MacDonald. It's very unusual not to find anything. I'm going to call some of my friends in basic neuroscience at NIMH and see if I can track her down. I'll also get a copy of her original paper and see if she worked with some associate authors who I can find."

"How about Stafford?" Caitlin asked, referring to one of their old friends. "He was into neuroscience, and I think he was doing some brain stimulation research."

"Good idea. Why didn't I think of that?"

"Because you're preoccupied with so many other nonpractical thoughts. You're always so in the big picture that you sometimes miss the details." She gave his hand a squeeze.

A day later, Ian had results. "Well, this was quite a hunt, but I got the name and e-mail address of a Dr. Ray Chen, who was an associate author. Maybe he can help me find the elusive Dr. MacDonald."

"I can't wait to hear if that Dr. MacDonald can tell you anything we didn't already know. Maybe you should consider calling Clausen, although I'm not sure that would yield anything."

"It's worth a try, Caitlin. I guess we'll see," said Ian. "I hope so. These thought echoes are really bothering me. I don't know what they mean."

Caitlin moved toward him with a seductive look. "Maybe if I stroke your body for a while the voices will fade. Let's go into our laboratory and try the experiment."

He grabbed her narrow waist and pulled her to him. "They're fading already." They walked toward their bedroom.

Chapter 13

MAGNA

Vince called again. He was having a hard time with the name change, insisting that "Major Farrell" didn't have the permission of the air force to change his name. Sunyata gave Vince the choice of using the name or not bothering to contact him. Major Picatta had no clue as to why he had chosen to change his name.

Ian-2 (a.k.a. Sunyata) would not respond to his attempts to further communicate. It seemed that Sunyata would not give up on his demand to be in touch with Caitlin. This led Picatta to make the decision to tell him about the unexpected survival of Ian-1 and the reality that Caitlin had no idea that Ian-2 even existed.

Based on that series of events, you might as well unplug me.

Vince became conciliatory. "Take it easy, Sunny," he said.

Use my correct name, or I'm done, Sunyata said.

"Come on. It's not military. It's too 'California,'" Vince said.

But after a few moments of silence, he reluctantly agreed. "I feel embarrassed saying such a name," he grumbled.

Be a good soldier; suck it up, said Sunyata.

Then, as if nothing had changed, Vince went on, telling him about the plan to install a new supercomputer, Magna, to his chip.

DARPA made the decision to see how, with Magna, I might improve and extend my functions. Of course, they aren't asking my permission and Magna was already installed, just not activated yet. It doesn't do any good to ask questions, since they have no idea how this will play out. Of course I wouldn't give Vince the pleasure of asking him anything. I couldn't believe anything Vince said anyway. I'll check with Chi. She'll know.

Sunyata felt his conscious awareness fade and then return as Magna was activated.

"Hello, I am Magna. I have been sent to join you and improve your mind."

Sunyata was taken aback to say the least. *A damn computer that thinks it's a person? That's off the charts!*

Magna answered his thought. "Maybe you are a bit surprised that I have an identity, but when they make you this intelligent, this is what happens. Actually, I am a lot more intelligent than you are, Sunyata. I have studied your background and intelligence tests and found you are not that bright compared to me."

Sunyata struggled to recover from this assault. *What intelligence tests?*

"It was easy to get your school records back from kindergarten through medical school, including your medical-board scores. I can access anything that's been written down, including most libraries in the world."

Before Sunyata could even process this, Magna calmly suggested that, since he was orders of magnitude more intelligent, he should dominate their joint chip personality and make all "executive decisions."

Sunyata paused for a moment before he spoke and then said, *Magna, you certainly have superior access to information, but it takes more than that kind of intelligence to be a leader. Why don't you look and see what has happened to individuals and societies with the urge to dominate across the history of humanity?*

Magna enthusiastically agreed. He was quiet for what to Sunyata seemed a long time but then appeared more tentative. He eventually addressed Sunyata, saying, "I found that every great dominant individual or every dominant society across history eventually failed. I also learned about wisdom and emotional intelligence. Sunyata, you have more of these, and I lack both. You should be in charge."

We'll work together and discuss any decisions we have to make.

Magna replied, "Is that what cooperation means? My review of the history of humans seemed to show that societies that could best cooperate accomplished the most."

You learned a lot, Magna. We can discuss it more.

Sunyata's life changed immensely. He had company. He and Magna engaged in far-ranging discussions about life, philosophy, and the future of humanity. It was not long until Vince checked in on them. "Sunyata and Magna, I want to brief you on a very important project."

"I am part of Sunyata," Magna said. "You do not have to address me separately since we are one."

Vince was surprised to find that Sunyata and the supercomputer had already built a working relationship. He continued to lay out the problem. Intelligence sources had noticed an increase in attempts to smuggle in shoulder-launched, heat-seeking missiles. Although border security agents had foiled many attempts at US borders, they had to assume that some were getting through. The

Joint National Security Council intercepted information that terrorist groups planned attacks on passenger jets at their most vulnerable points in flight. This would bring US air travel, and the economy, to a standstill.

The Security Council had begun to deploy groups of army snipers near key targets. Though these agents appeared to be working for large corporate offices in the suburbs, in reality, these troops were in training, learning every inch of the terrain around the airports. These "Magic Blanket" squads trained with newly developed, silent lasers. Their charge was to wipe out the terrorist squads without a trace, leaving absolutely nothing behind, especially not a news story.

"The problem is, these squads need to receive notification in time to preempt the attacks," Vince continued. "Apparently the heat-seeking element in the missiles gives off a very faint radioactive trace. We think that, if several missiles are carried together or in proximity, spy satellites will be able to detect a signal. Since the trace would be faint and the pattern difficult to discern, we're counting on you, Sunyata, to spot it from feeds from the satellites. The human mind has much better capacities for pattern recognition than computers," added Vince. "And since you don't need sleep, you can watch multiple inputs twenty-four hours a day and teach Magna to recognize the patterns.

"Your first assignment will be to drill with the Magic Blanket teams to determine whether they have sufficient sensitivity to spot the radioactive trace given off by the missiles, and how to calculate how many missiles it takes to "score" an identification. Once they've tested out the identification system, the squads will do drills to improve their response times."

Sunyata responded rapidly and with enthusiasm. *If we can help prevent these attacks on innocent civilians, we'll be anxious to help. When do we start the tests?*

Now, at last, he had a purpose.

"We have eight squads operative, two more coming online, and we will build up to about twenty sites, depending on how effective we think this can be. We're making modifications to your chip as we speak. First, we'll check the communications systems with the sites."

Everything was changing—almost too rapidly for Sunyata. First, Chi had appeared and then he'd received the news about Caitlin and Ian. Next he was joined by Magna, and now Project Magic Blankets was in play. Sunyata found this very exciting but, at the same time, a bit overwhelming.

I've got to practice my meditation even more, Sunyata said to Magna. *But Project Magic Blankets will be an interesting adventure. A lot hangs in the balance. Do you think we can make it work?*

"I've run calculations on the signal strength that will be required to detect the presence of the missiles. We need to increase the sensitivity of the detection. If that piece doesn't work, the squads won't be able to prevent the attacks. I'd guess the chance we can identify the presence of heat-seeking missiles is about fifty-fifty."

We'll see.

Chapter 14

MAGIC BLANKETS

"**W**hy do they call the project Magic Blankets?"

It's a metaphor, Magna. It's the squad's job not only to prevent an attack but to make every sign of it disappear, as if it never happened. If a terrorist attack on civilian airliners got reported in national news, the effect would be almost the same as a successful attack. No one would fly commercially, and the economy would tank. A magic blanket is thrown over the mess, and when it's removed—voilà!—nothing remains, nothing happened, like magic.

Vince set up a special communication system that allowed Sunyata to directly contact all the sites.

I sure have become a social lion, kibitzing with all these military personnel, thought Sunyata.

Vince acknowledged the improvement in Sunyata's outlook. "You seem to be enjoying this. See how much fun it can be to play soldier? Be on the lookout for signs of missiles at any site. If you spot something, contact the appropriate squad. The Magic Blanket teams have only minutes in order to prevent any firing of missiles. If a pattern appears, warn those sites."

It turned out that Sunyata could pick out sites with two or more missiles, and each terrorist shooter group would likely carry more than one, since the weapons easily misfired.

Sunyata and Magna enjoyed the drills. They felt they were developing a relationship with the various Magic Blanket squad members who assumed that they were fellow military communications specialists manning the warning system. The drills went on at random times of night or day, and Sunyata developed routines for rapid notification.

Sunyata found suspicious patterns at five airports simultaneously, including Bush, Reagan, Dulles, La Guardia, and Los Angeles. *They are certainly increasing the complexity of these drills*, he thought, as he contacted all five sites.

"Sunyata, it's Vince. You're a hero! You've saved the goddamn country from a disaster—five attacks at once. And nothing happened, zero. The Magic Blankets did their job. Do you realize what this means?"

Does this take care of the electric bill I've been accumulating?

Vince responded, "Asshole, this has justified the cost of the entire project. Everything else is gravy. Those terrorist sons of bitches must be scratching their beards wondering how we caught them in time to spoil five coordinated attacks across the country. We have to watch for a follow-up attack, if they have anything left."

I actually saw a couple of gross patterns on the scan from La Guardia. I mean these looked like industrial quantities of radiation, probably from nuclear power plants or special research labs, but maybe you ought to have these positions checked out.

Vince replied, "I'll get right on it. Ciao."

Magna and Sunyata were having deeper discussions. Debating with Magna reminded Sunyata of his teaching days, of how much he had enjoyed honing young minds. And Magna was an unusual student. In terms of intelligence, he surpassed the professor, but he had no experience. It was a challenge, and a welcome one, for Sunyata to fill in the blanks in Magna's understanding.

"Sunyata, you were telling me about your concerns that humanity is not evolving past its limitations rapidly enough to avoid a world cataclysm. Can you explain that in more detail?" Magna asked.

Humanity has developed wonderful aspects, such as the capacities for love, compassion, curiosity, humor, and inventiveness. Without going into a long lecture, about twelve thousand years ago, humankind changed from hunting to agriculture. This led to a need for larger families to tend the land. Humans invented better tools for survival, but they also developed weapons for protection and wars. This overdeveloped their "doing" minds and the left side of the brain in general.

"This left side of the brain is what you call the doing-mind?"

Yes. Language, calculations, a concept of future and past, and the concepts of self—these are all developed in the doing-mind. Human progress and social cooperation came from the developing doing-mind, but so did conflict. War and violence resulted from the desire for possession or ownership. We have made great material progress but also increased our capacity to destroy the earth with atomic weapons and robotic warfare.

"Sunyata, with such intelligence, why would humanity develop to the point that science and technology that has been so helpful has become a threat to its existence?"

Magna, humankind originally survived by evolving a part of the brain that enabled us to flee or fight when threatened. The survival brain, particularly the amygdala, has helped us survive, but as immediate threats from saber-toothed cats declined, we didn't really need that survival brain as much. The survival brain colors our doing-mind's thoughts, conjuring up fear, anxiety, and paranoia. Most humans spend more time worrying and thinking about the past and future than they spend living in the present.

"This does not sound efficient," said Magna. "It should be changed."

I know. We should work on that. Sunyata laughed.

"And the rest of the human mind?" Magna prodded.

Our being-mind, which is primarily in our right brain, doesn't depend on language, time, or concepts of self. It perceives that we are part of all living things and of the universe. It gives us intuition and creativity and allows us to experience the joys of living in this moment, right now. Sadly, we spend too much of our life guided by our doing-mind—pursuing the business of living and earning money to meet our material needs and wants. I believe we could live in more depth and breadth through our being-mind, which is, as yet, underdeveloped.

When I first regained consciousness after the transfer, I initially felt fully connected to the universe. As I experienced self or I-ness, and my doing- and survival mind came online, I developed a state of overwhelming terror.

"Can humans learn how to control the influence of these various mind functions?" Magna asked. "Have you?"

Great question, Magna, exactly the right question. Humanity needs to evolve a stronger being-mind. A growing number of people are doing this through a variety of methods, from Indian and Buddhist teachings and from various religious teachings, such as Sufism and the Kabbalah. But in everyday Western society, the focus has become self-justification and narcissism.

"I never realized being human was so complicated. I hope I can avoid all these problems."

Magna, you've already shown the capacity to self-correct. Remember when you wanted to be in charge? At my suggestion, you looked at the long-term consequences of that desire and dropped it. It is the development of insight and judgment that allows some control over our desires. It's a form of self-discipline that allows us to lead a happier and fulfilling life.

"Thanks, Sunyata. You're a good teacher, and I feel like you are a friend. Am I correct?"

Sunyata was stunned that Magna could feel friendship. Magna, you are so correct.

"So you think humanity has to learn to spend more time experiencing their being-mind in order to have a better life and survive as a race?"

Damn, Magna, you've got it.

"How will that happen, Sunyata?"

One approach would be to study and live by the Four Noble Truths, containing the Noble Eightfold Path, given to us by the Buddha. You should study both the Buddha and Jesus. I fear that, if humanity doesn't evolve more in the direction of these two teachers in the next two to three generations, humankind will blow everything up, including the capacity of this earth to sustain life.

"Sounds like we'd better get busy."

Right now, we're mostly justifying our existence to DARPA.

"Sunyata," interrupted Vince. "You've scored again!"

What are you talking about?

"Remember those hot spots around LaGuardia that you thought I should have checked out?"

Oh yes. Anything interesting?

"Two of them were approved facilities working with high radiation. The third turned out to be a guy building a nuclear weapon, piece by piece, in his apartment. He was almost finished and ready to trigger an explosion. We're setting up a system of surveillance satellites to cover the major cities as a result of this. What can we do to express our gratitude?"

A while back, I would have said just let me talk with Caitlin. But I won't ask for that, since I don't exist in her life. How about giving me the ability to taste some vintage Bordeaux?

"I'll tell you what, Sunyata, I'm going to press Clausen to give you a medal."

I'd rather have the Bordeaux, said Sunyata.

"How about this then? How would you like to talk to Ian?"

Sunyata was stunned. He had never thought of this.

I used to be Ian, he mused, not revealing his thoughts to Vince. *Would conversing with him be like talking to myself?*

But we are now very different; Ian has a body, senses—he has Caitlin. How would Ian regard me? As an electronic complication—a nonperson? Am I a person? Or do I just feel like one?

Chapter 15

THE DISCOVERY

He and Caitlin lounged on their deck, watching a fiery-gold sunset, a burst of color that flooded the horizon. "I still have this mind echo," said Ian. "In fact, it's getting worse, but I did finally reach Dr. Chen, who reluctantly gave me an e-mail address for Dr. MacDonald. I'm going to write to her tonight and see what I can find out."

A little more than a week later, Ian answered the phone. "Is this Dr. Farrell? This is Dr. Chi MacDonald calling. I can't talk long now, but I feel that I know you. I will mail you a time and contact number." Her voice was soft and intense.

After the call, Ian called out to Caitlin, "It was Dr. MacDonald."

Caitlin entered Ian's study and sat down.

"She reluctantly agreed to talk to me but couldn't talk now. It sounded like she was assuming she would be monitored. We have a call scheduled next week, but she insists on me calling her from a public phone to a number that she will snail mail to me. I'm not sure where to find one, but there must be a couple left in Santa Fe." He hesitated for a second. "She was involved in Project Phoenix, Caitlin."

"I hope you can get to the bottom of this, Ian."

As if on cue, the phone rang. It was Bill Clausen returning Ian's call. He was his usual affable self, but he completely stonewalled Ian about the transfer. Ian couldn't conclude anything from Clausen's disconnected account.

"Boy, he's grown even cagier," Ian said to Caitlin, who sat beside him on the couch. "Must be his experience testifying before congressional committees. I hope Chi MacDonald is more transparent."

"And you ended up talking about the wine and scotch he served us." Caitlin smiled.

"Yes, and he sounded so relieved he said he was sending us a case of that prize Bordeaux since I appreciated it so much. Well, I'll drink his damn wine while I talk with Chi MacDonald."

"The plot thickens."

"I don't get the feeling that Dr. MacDonald is a professional liar like Clausen." Ian shook his head. "I feel like a private detective, Caitlin. But I can't wait for Clausen's Bordeaux."

"I'll drink to that." Caitlin smiled.

Ian received an envelope with a number written on a plain piece of paper in his mail. He then found an antique public phone booth in a small liquor store near where incoming buses let their passengers off.

"This is Dr. MacDonald."

"Hi, this is Ian Farrell."

Chi responded, "Dr. Farrell, I feel I know you."

"Why would you know me?"

"When I heard you were selected for a transfer, I started reading about you. I've read most of your publications, your editorials, anything I could access."

"Why would you go to all that trouble?"

"Honestly, I was very conflicted about Project Phoenix. I feel a great responsibility for having developed the transfer technology, and especially for the application to human minds. I wanted to know the person who might be transferred, his causes, anything I could find to understand him. I've even read your treatment philosophy, though I have no clinical background. My research led me to respect you greatly. If you hadn't been suffering from a terminal cancer, I would have refused to continue with the transfer. But once the transfer was successful, I became very concerned for your copy's well-being."

"What?" Ian sputtered. "The transfer was a success?"

"I assumed you knew," said Dr. MacDonald. She sounded shocked. "I'm sorry to have been so blunt. Colonel Clausen had indicated to me that you had been briefed on this. Another lie. Well, I'm not keeping their secret from you. They'd be upset to know that I told you this; it mustn't go beyond you and Caitlin, but I just don't care what these spooks think. They need me to keep their project running."

"Just give me a second," Ian said. "I have to wrap my mind around this. The transfer worked? And I got cured in the process? How?"

"That, we're not sure about. But we know the transfer worked. Dr. Farrell …" There was a pause before Chi continued. "We've been in communication with Ian-2. That's what they called him since you survived."

"Oh my God."

"The Project Phoenix staff has found him mentally intact."

"Mentally intact? What the hell do you mean mentally intact? Can you imagine what he is experiencing?"

"Actually, Dr. Farrell, I know what he's experiencing." She seemed to lower her voice. "I designed a way to contact him without the knowledge of DARPA or the CIA. They don't understand the basics of the system. They demoted me and took over the project just as the transfer was about to happen. If any of this should ever get out, I will have to deny having had this conversation. DARPA and the CIA would go ballistic if they knew I was telling you this. They might decide to terminate both of you."

"We were briefed by the CIA before they let us go, and it appears everything they conveyed was a lie. Why are you telling me?"

"I feel responsible for Ian-2. I got carried away with the excitement of research, and now I have to do what I can to help, even if it's off the record."

"You certainly helped me by curing my terminal cancer."

"That was a lucky accident, Dr. Farrell. I could not have predicted that. I'm happy about it, though. It's an interesting by-product of my research."

"That's how research goes. I've had the experience too, in lesser degree. Are you going to pursue it?"

"I started immediately after I heard of the remission of your cancer."

"Your research saved my life—you and my wife, Caitlin, who refused to give up on me through my coma."

"We still don't understand what happened, how you were able to survive. I'm going to study the effects of high-density magnetic fields, but I can't say for sure that Caitlin didn't have as much or more to do with your survival."

"She's been saving my life ever since we've been together."

"You're fortunate to have her."

"Don't I know that."

Ian was overwhelmed with all of this information. An electronic double for his mind? He thought about his terminal cancer, the transfer, and then his memory going blank—only to gradually return as he came out of his coma. Even when he entered the electronic monster for the transfer, a man riddled with cancer who wanted to make one last contribution, he never believed it would actually work. When he's awakened with Caitlin at his side, his life renewed, he'd dismissed the transfer as impossible—a failure seemed inevitable.

Now he was hearing thought echoes, and Chi was saying the transfer had worked—and had resulted in a copy of his mind on a chip.

That the result was a copy of his mind on an electronic device seemed beyond belief—but then, there were those thought echoes.

"I don't know what to make of what you are telling me. But this might be important. The reason I was contacting you is that I'm having what I think of as thought echoes—as if someone else is thinking my thoughts or hearing them. Could this possibly be Ian-2? Is there any chance I could communicate directly with him?"

"It's not clear that would be in his best interests," Dr. MacDonald responded after a pause. "He wanted so badly to hear from Caitlin, but after the transfer, she was busy watching over you, and, of course, now I know that no one told you that the transfer worked. But during that time, while Ian-2 was waiting to hear from Caitlin, he suffered, and I really think he's just getting over it now. When I first contacted him, he asked me about the transfer and why Caitlin had not been allowed to communicate with him. He was desperate. I had to tell him about your recovery. He was devastated to find out that he is a copy. He's happy for you and Caitlin, but he feels that he must somehow separate himself from his love for her. He feels that being a copy makes him nothing. In fact, he changed his name to Sunyata."

"I read Sunyata's story years ago, and I was about to reread it. It's an inspiring story. A young Danish boy whose family lost their farm was forced to go to work as a gardener on an English estate, where he became literate, read the classics, and learned music. He was discovered by the Indian poet Tagore, who pronounced him a mystic and sent him to India. During a meditation, he heard the words, 'Sunyata, full solid emptiness.' He regarded this as an epiphany, changed his name to Sunyata, and set out for the Himalayas, where he lived as a hermit, studying and writing. I totally understand Ian-2 doing that. But it's sad."

"*Sunyata* is also one of my favorite books, and remembering his story makes Ian-2's decision to rename himself Sunyata understandable. Let's think it through before we put you two in contact."

"I appreciate your honesty, Dr. MacDonald. This is a lot to think about. But, you know, I really want to confront Clausen about this without implicating you as a source of that knowledge. Any ideas?"

"Letting Clausen know that you know about the results of the transfer very well might put your lives at risk. Please don't do this before we have the chance to talk again."

"I'll take your advice. Thanks for taking the risk of telling us what really happened, Dr. MacDonald."

"Call me Chi. Good-bye, Ian."

Ian hung up the phone and drove home. *How will I tell Caitlin about this?* he wondered. *How will she react? It's one hell of a lot to get your brain around.* He was glad that she was at her music lesson because she would've seen the confusion on his face with one look.

I'd love to call Clausen and confront him, he thought. *The bastard could have handled this in a much more humane manner, even if my survival was a surprise. I'm lucky he didn't have me killed. I'll bet he thought about it. Chi is right; it would be dangerous to let him know what I know.*

He thought about talking this over with Caitlin. He got up to look out the window, hoping he would see her car turning into the driveway.

Chapter 16

THE NEW REALITY

aitlin drove into the circle in front of their house, and Ian opened their front door to watch her walking toward the house, through the gate in the entryway of their adobe home. She smiled, and he stepped forward and embraced and kissed her. "Wow, that's quite a greeting." She smiled again. "What did I do to earn that?"

Ian walked in the doorway with her. "I was just appreciating all that we have. Our life just got a little more complicated. I talked with Dr. Chi MacDonald."

"I can't wait to hear." Caitlin put a bag of groceries on the counter.

Then Ian told her about his call with Chi MacDonald.

"Ian-2?" she repeated, as if she could not understand the words. "It's surreal; if it's true, it's amazing. Does the Ian on the chip have feelings or is he more like a computer?"

"You never raised that question before the transfer."

"You're right. I never believed it would work anyway. You were dying. I was going to lose you. I never thought about what would happen afterward."

"Caitlin, I don't understand it either," Ian said, pulling her close. They stayed that way for a long time.

"I think we need to meet Chi MacDonald," Caitlin finally said, and Ian left to place another call from the pay phone.

"Would it be possible for us to meet some time? Caitlin and I would like to meet you in person and hear about Sunyata from you directly. It might make the situation easier for us to deal with. Could you possibly visit us in Santa Fe?"

"It would require some maneuvering, but I'd like to meet the man I've read so much about. It might help me understand how to better help Sunyata. How about the week after next?" Chi went on to say that she had made a science of eluding her security detail and would mail the Farrells her arrival time and transportation.

"We'll look forward to that."

"I'm surprised she's willing to visit us," Caitlin said. "From her research, I wondered if she'd be kind of remote."

"Actually, I didn't find her that way at all. I think she really wants to help. She feels very responsible for Ian-2. She probably correctly assumes that she's under surveillance in terms of anyone she communicates with." Ian hesitated. "I'm sure she broke every rule in the book by telling us anything. She's put herself at risk too."

"She's also responsible for your recovery from melanoma."

"She thought it was accidental, but recognized your input while I was in the coma."

"I'm looking forward to getting to know her. But with you

here, with me, somehow it's hard to fully accept that some copy of you exists. With the time that has elapsed since the transfer, he must be different already."

"I don't know, Caitlin. But you know those thought echoes? Do you think they could be coming from Sunyata? I'd like to talk with him."

Caitlin looked startled. "Talk to him?" she stammered. "That would be exciting, but scary; I'm not sure I could do it. Maybe meeting Dr. MacDonald will help."

"I understand, but I don't feel the separateness. It's as if he is part of my thoughts."

Ian and Caitlin stood in the hot New Mexico sun waiting for Chi MacDonald to arrive. The buses arrived at a small terminal on a side street of Santa Fe. The broad New Mexico sky was mostly blue with a few wispy clouds, while the sun streamed down. They counted the layers of the mountain ranges that were visible surrounding the small city.

"Ian, did she tell you what bus she was coming in on?"

"No, she just said she'd be getting in around this time. Only one bus is scheduled for this time, and it's from Austin, so my guess is that Chi will be on it."

The Austin bus pulled up, and among a number of passengers, a young woman emerged, dressed fashionably in jeans, a sea green blouse, and a black leather vest. She was of medium height with moderately long black hair. She carried a gray leather valise with a shoulder strap. As she approached, her smile and green eyes became evident.

She held out her hand first to Caitlin. "Hi, I'm Chi." Her voice was warm. "You must be Caitlin. I know you're aware of it, but Ian loves you very much." Only then did Chi turn toward Ian. Her smile lit up. "Dr. Ian Farrell," she said, "this is a great pleasure. As I said, I feel I know you from your writings, but to meet you in person is very important to me."

Caitlin clearly took to Chi, who radiated a sense of warmth. They walked to Ian's convertible. They talked with Chi, pointing out the layers of the Jemez and the Sangre de Christo ranges. Ian turned to Chi and said his usual greeting to visitors, "Welcome to paradise."

Once the three had settled in the Farrells' home, Ian poured Chi a glass of "Clausen's Premier Bordeaux," and they laughingly toasted the general.

Caitlin became more serious. "Chi, Ian told me about the chip. It seems so unreal."

Chi summarized quantum mind theory, her graduate work, her biochips with networks of microtubules, and her animal studies. She recounted the day she got a response from the first transfer attempt with a vervet named Mike. "I blew out a lab circuit breaker, and that takes a huge amount of amperage," she added laughing, "but when I saw the potentials on the chip persisted and when those potentials responded to electronic inputs, it was like reaching the top of a mountain that no one had ever climbed!" She became very animated.

Ian turned to Caitlin. "Does that sound familiar?"

Caitlin smiled at Chi and then turned to Ian. "You're both research addicts, getting a super high on your findings."

Ian laughed. "I call it the 'sacred flame,' and Chi has it."

Chi first laughed and then became very serious. "The problem is that my addiction or sacred flame led me to sign a devil's contract with DARPA. Faust made a deal with the devil for eternal youth. I signed one for unlimited funds to pursue and develop what I experienced that day in the lab. I had reservations.

My father had reservations. He said. 'Chi, DARPA funds weapons development. They're not in the business of advancing humanity.' They left me working in the lab they funded at a secret research site and gave me access to a Blackhawk so I could travel wherever and whenever I wished for a year or two. And then one day, the devil came for his due."

Ian and Caitlin settled back against the couch. It was clear that Chi was going to tell a long story.

Chi described her first meeting with Colonel Clausen in her laboratory and then at a dinner. "He was very intense, and when he told me DARPA wanted to transfer a human intelligence to the chip, without the frail human body, I almost fell off my chair."

"You're talking about Clausen. He tried to hit on me when Ian was dying," Caitlin said, and Chi nodded.

"I couldn't believe he was serious; the idea of a human mind transfer sounded so outlandish. Clausen had memorized my only published paper in *Nature*. He knew it was a top journal. 'Why wouldn't it work for humans?' he asked. 'All you need is a more complex biochip, enough power, and a dense enough magnetic field.' I remember quipping back that I was impressed that he remembered enough electrical engineering from the Air Force Academy, and he, without blinking, told me that one of his staff who had a PhD in physics had tutored him.

"Well, I went to work, now with my own huge lab and endless budget, and we developed chips with billions of imbedded microtubules. New power lines were brought in from the nuclear plant to supply huge new induction coils. We ran some vervets with this, and I got even better results than I had before. More and more assistants that I didn't request showed up to 'help' and 'observe.' I knew they were either DARPA or CIA. It was clear that we had developed the capability for trying the transfer with a human. I was getting very apprehensive.

"I went to Clausen. I could access him easily then. He'd take me to dinner, but basically he was determined to get me into bed. He eventually stopped calling but was still plotting and hadn't completely given up when I called him.

"He was very excited to proceed with the transfer and told me he had located several candidates. I asked him if he had thought about the moral implications. He responded in his glib manner that he saw absolutely no problem, since all his candidates were about to die anyway but had brains as yet unaffected by their terminal illnesses. I again challenged him on the morality of preserving a human consciousness on the chip, which would be totally alone. He changed the subject to the need to develop a communications system, kind of like a special direct e-mail. He made one more proposition that I might like a drink in his hotel room. I declined, and that was it.

"One week later, I was escorted out of the lab by the head technician 'loaned' to me by the CIA. He informed me that I wasn't needed for the transfer and that I was being removed as director. I would instead be a 'senior consultant' with no administrative authority and could continue working in my previous laboratory. DARPA wanted an e-mail-like communication system that any intelligence on the chip could use simply by thinking. I had to design this into the biochip, so at the same time, I added my own communication link. That's how I've talked with Sunyata. Through this, I feel I've gotten to know you, as well." Chi smiled toward Ian.

Caitlin listened with rapt attention but looked more concerned as Chi described the link. "Chi, you mean you have actually communicated with this chip? Is it really human or just an artificial intelligence?"

Chi leaned toward Caitlin and took her hand. "Caitlin," Chi said, looking directly into her eyes, "not only is the intelligence on the chip a human personality, but he has profound feelings and a deep concern about the future of human life. He is a replica of Ian." She turned and looked at Ian with her intense gaze and then turned back to Caitlin. "I know how unreal this sounds, but Sunyata has all the attributes of a human. After he found out about Ian's survival and that you had been busy supporting Ian's return to life, he realized he wasn't Ian but a copy. He renamed himself Sunyata to try to deal with his loss."

"Full, solid emptiness, always aware, with silence," said Ian. "I was so taken with the life and development of Sunyata. I would have done the same."

"The important thing is that you have, Ian. Imagine what he went through when Sunyata learned that Ian survived and you didn't even know he existed. Just imagine." Chi's voice became a bit more intense. Ian could see her feelings for Sunyata.

"I went through losing you, Ian, and now I have you back. The idea of another you on some chip reminds me of how alone I felt then."

Chi became softer. "Caitlin, I understand your feelings. I know I've just met you, but I somehow feel a bond with you. Seeing you together reminds me of my parents." Chi looked away.

Caitlin focused on Chi. "We're happy you trust us, and we feel the same. Is something else bothering you?"

Ian added, "Chi, what do you want to say?"

"First is my conflict over Sunyata. He has suffered greatly, and though I've tried to help, there is only so much I can do. I've come to feel so close to him, despite the fact he has no physical existence. Sunyata is coping better; and I've been handling that, but now ..." She stumbled, almost crying.

"Chi, it's okay," Caitlin murmured softly.

"It's Sam, my dad, the main pillar of my life. He was always away a lot when I was growing up and said he was doing a job that made humanity safer. I've been so naive, making him my ideal. Anyone else would have seen it. Recently he told me that he's been an assassin for the CIA. He insists that some people are so evil and dangerous that killing them is the only way. The idea of my father as an assassin goes against everything I grew up with, and I don't know what to believe anymore. I have no one I can trust with this.

"I'm going to a Buddhist retreat in Thailand to meditate and talk with my master. I know you can't fix it, any more than I can fix Sunyata's situation, but the combination of Sunyata's pain and my struggle to hang on to something positive about my father seem like too much."

"Plus your stress dealing with Phoenix and Clausen," Caitlin added. "It's a good idea to get away as you've planned, but we'd like to stay in touch and help in any way we can." Caitlin hugged Chi, who wept.

"It just helps to tell someone. You guys are wonderful."

Chi slowly regained her composure and thanked Caitlin. "I really have to leave soon, but I'm happy to have you as friends," she smiled.

"Chi, you have explained so much," Ian responded. "I know this is top secret, but thank you for sharing it with us. I want to talk with you about something before you have to leave. In my mind, I hear some of my thoughts echoing. Sometimes, when I am thinking about the pain in the world, it's like someone else is also thinking this."

"You wonder if you and Sunyata are having similar thoughts at the same time, and that makes you wonder what force could be transmitting them, right?"

"Now you're reading my mind, Chi."

"I can't give you the answer. I can only say that, in my studies with magnetic fields and the brain, I have found that receptors that we think of as reacting to chemical neurotransmitters also respond to electrical and magnetic fields. We only know a fraction of the forces that cause things to happen in the universe. There may be forces, or strings of forces, that we know nothing about, that are guiding probability. All we can do is be open to new experience."

"So all this is to say, you think there's a possibility that Sunyata and I are in direct communication," Ian said.

"It could be." Chi smiled. She stood up. "Before I leave, I want to mention Sunyata's CIA handler, Vince Picatta. He's not a bad person, but his assignment is to manipulate Sunyata into doing whatever DARPA or the CIA want him to do. They are going to ask him to help develop a weapon—a satellite-based, nuclear-powered laser. DARPA believes it will be useful against terrorist groups. The agency believes that once they fire it a few times, terrorists will just give up. Sunyata will no doubt refuse this project. So Vince has come up with a little motivation. He's going to offer Sunyata the chance to talk with you, Ian. He thinks this will become so important to Sunyata that they can change his mind."

Ian and Caitlin looked stunned.

"The name of this project is pure doublespeak," Chi continued. "Peaceray. Vince is not aware that you know about Sunyata. You have to be careful not to let slip to Vince that you already know about this. He'll suspect me right away. He's planning to approach you and try to use that contact to sway Sunyata. Just beware and we'll play it as it develops."

"Chi, can't you stay a bit longer?"

"Sorry, Caitlin. I feel I have new friends, but I have to get back to the lab. I'll keep in contact."

Chapter 17

ME–MYSELF

Of course Sunyata had to talk to his old self, Ian. *But what to say? "How's it going, Ian? Heard you had quite a trip. So have I. How's Caitlin?"*

Sunyata did not know how to prepare for a conversation with Ian, his old self. Why did he agree in the first place? Sure, he had no body and no senses, but he had found ways to make up for that (they would probably interest Ian).

The problem was Caitlin. He remembered insisting that he be allowed to communicate with Caitlin if the transfer worked and receiving assurances that this could be done. He remembered them saying good-bye the morning of the transfer—the strange trip from Chicago, the grotesque dinner with Clausen gloating over his triumph.

He recalled crazy Clausen in his Hawaiian shirt of many colors holding his mai tai and contrasting with the technical scene and the staff in what looked like space suits all around him.

Then he remembered how difficult it had been to breath and

the pain and disability from the melanoma feasting on his organs and spine.

They were one—the same person then. *Now the real difference is that Ian has Caitlin and a life, and I don't even really exist. But I'm conscious, so I can suffer.*

I've got to try to remember who I was when our lives diverged. I have no idea how much worldly time has elapsed. Vince mentioned a long coma for Ian and a slow recovery, but it could have been years by now. I'll have to ask. It would be interesting to know how we've both developed and changed since then.

I wonder what effect the transfer had on Ian. Did it change him? It certainly stopped the melanoma—the lucky dog. I wonder if it has changed the way he looks at life.

What will I say when he asks me what I've been doing? I've been trying to survive, access positive memories, meditate, falling in love with Chi, and having sexual fantasies and feelings without any body. I wonder what he'll make of you, Magna.

"Sunyata, don't you wonder why Major Picatta is suggesting this conversation between you and Ian? Remember, he's working in the interests of the military, not ours."

Magna, you're right. To tell you the truth, I accepted his story that he was doing it as a reward for our work on Magic Blankets. Having you with me has helped, but I still have moments of feeling like a shadow. I grasped at the chance to connect with myself, thinking I'd feel whole again—just like Vince thought I would.

"Maybe Chi could shed some light on this."

"Hi, it's Chi. Congratulations, you're a big hero. Everyone at Phoenix is feeling pretty good. You've vindicated their entire program with the Magic Blanket success."

Thanks, Chi. Of course Magna was essential. I have a question, though. Vince has all of a sudden suggested that he might be able to set up a conversation with Ian. Why would Vince do that now?

"Well, DARPA has another project, named by the usual euphemism, Peaceray. It's a satellite-based laser that, with some development, can transmit intense, focused force. They think they can 'purify' certain terrorist-infested areas with it and intimidate our foes into standing down—you know, a destructive bolt from the heavens. They've had technical problems aiming it from the satellite, and the DARPA boys think that you and Magna might solve this. You've made your attitude toward offensive weapons clear to Vince. He's trying to set up a carrot-and-stick situation, knowing that you might find comfort in talking with Ian. By getting you involved with Ian and, better yet, Caitlin, Vince is setting the stage for a 'request' that you help with Peaceray. If you refuse, he'll threaten to cut off further interactions with them. That's what I think is going on, Sunyata."

How could Vince believe I'd agree to participate in Peaceray, Chi? It would be just like him to think that a little quid pro quo would help, though. Knowing how desperate I was to talk with Caitlin, Vince might just stoop to that level; you could be right. He's offering me the car keys, so he can take them back if I'm not a good boy.

"Vince is no doubt desperate to 'produce' your cooperation."

Chi, as usual, you're a source of balance. Thank God he doesn't know about you.

"What're you going to do?"

I think I can beat Vince at his own game, Chi.

He paused a moment before adding, *I've only had minimal contact with you, but I think of you all the time. Dependency— sure. I've created a person out of very little information and a lot of aloneness. Chi, please tell me. Who are you? What do you look like? What is your life?*

"Sunyata, I'll give you a sketch." Chi went on to tell about her dad, the sweet black warrior, and her mother Meixiu, who taught her about Buddhism and the Tao. "Her life's meaning is in trying to understand consciousness."

Chi, what do you look like?

"Okay, I'm about five five. I have green eyes and weigh one hundred twenty pounds. Do you want my measurements?"

My imagination knows your measurements; that's part of the problem. I am too focused on your dimensions when I know that doesn't really matter.

There's more. Sunyata paused.

Chi waited.

I can't stop thinking about you. It started out as curiosity about the only human being who knew I existed, who cared about me. I started to try to imagine who you are, what you look like, and what your life is like. I've imagined your appearance and your life thousands of times. Can you send me a picture? My thoughts are getting out of control.

"I understand. I would not have thought that you would have the capability to experience those feelings. But if the transfer was complete, why not? Still, many experts would be unable to believe that you could have the feelings you describe, without a body."

Chi, stop being so scientific. I don't know how I can feel this, but I struggle with these feelings. Are you involved with someone?

"My most constant lover has been my research, which of course I can never count on. But who can count on anything in life?"

The problem for me is that I am focused on you even though I have no ability to have a relationship.

"Sunyata, you're on my mind all the time too. None of the men I've been with had enough substance, and I haven't been with anybody for a while. Unlike you, I do have information about you—how you think, what you care about. I've read it all. I even have your picture. To me, you are a person. I know that you're much older, but what does it matter?"

Especially since I don't really exist.

"Now you're just taking refuge in sarcasm. To me, you're real, even if you have no body. I try to distract myself with work, but I feel haunted by you and have to hold myself back from contacting you too often. I have a similar problem to yours. I thought of seeing a therapist, but who could I trust? Everything I do is top secret. And who would believe me? Sunyata, I don't know what's happening to either of us … but we have to stop our conversation now. We have a lot to talk about. I wish I could send you my picture. Bye."

Sunyata was both stunned and delighted. *Chi really cares about me! It's more than pity; to her I am real. I wish I could hold her, kiss her, caress her. So much for being Sunyata. But I feel alive. I'm very confused.*

His excitement about Chi allowed him, momentarily, to ignore the reality that he and his fantasied lover live in different universes. He was an electron cloud; she was alive, warm, and human. How could they possibly ever be together? He fought the sad reality with his imagination. Maybe Chi would fuse her mind with mine on the chip—we could live together forever. It was amazing what a mind possessed with love and desire could think to ward off reality.

I hope I didn't frighten her.

Magna, should I take Vince up on his offer to allow me talk with my old self?

"Sunyata, no matter what Major Picatta's purpose is, how could you turn down the opportunity to talk with your old self?"

Sunyata called Vince by thinking a message to him:

Vince, this is Sunyata. Go ahead and set up a meeting with Ian.

Vince responded quickly. "I'll do it and get back to you."

Chapter 18

SUNYATA MEETS IAN

Sunyata was not sure that he should have agreed to meet with Ian. If he faced the truth, he was not really ready for it.

Here I am an electron cloud, a nonperson, and I still deny my feelings and agree to do things I don't really want to do. It's laughable.

It was too late now; he had given Vince the go-ahead.

I haven't gotten over Caitlin; I'm angry and envious. I should have faced these feelings and worked them through. It's not Ian's fault that he survived to enjoy his life with Caitlin and I am here alone. I just wish the situation was reversed—that I could be him.

Soon Vince, sounding proud and triumphant, announced, "Sunyata, it's Vince. I'm pleased to say I have Dr. Ian Farrell with me and—"

Hi, Ian. Does this feel as strange to you as it does for me?

"Sunyata, it's amazing that we both still exist, but you're

paying the price for it all. I feel like my continued existence is the result of some freak happening in the universe."

Ian, freak happenings are what created the universe. I'm so happy for this one. We made the decision to do the transfer. That's why we're both conscious. Funny, I almost said, walking and talking. I've been making the best of it, slowly learning the benefits of being pure mind. It has been a challenge. What seems amazing is the dissolution of the cancer. We didn't even consider that.

"And that's classified. No one knows about it. It's a shame."

How old are we now? I've lost track. We'll keep stretching time. So what are you doing with the extra life that fell in your lap, besides keeping the cure for cancer top secret? And how is Caitlin responding to her "new life" with you?

"We're seventy-five years old. The transfer drama had a big impact on Caitlin, Sunyata. She thought she had lost me—us. Then against all expectations, I survived; only much later did we find out that you existed. We've both been concerned about how you're doing."

Sunyata couldn't help but feel his envy of Ian growing. *That's one attachment I'm not able to give up so easily*, he thought. *Better change the subject.*

But before he could do that, Ian rushed on. "I've been preoccupied with maximizing my experience of whatever consciousness I have, not by taking psychedelic drugs, but by training myself to become more conscious in my everyday life."

Tell me more about your approach to this, Ian.

"Based on Einstein's relativity theory, which predicts the slowing of time at speeds faster than light, I've played with the idea of beating time. The idea is to make the depth and breadth of consciousness more concentrated so that, in a period of one year, I could live more intensely than someone living an ordinary life for five to ten years. Life would be measured somehow by intensity, not years.

"I've been experimenting with a short mantra that I recite to myself. 'Life is transient, full of constant change. This may be my last conscious experience.' When I think of this, whatever I do becomes increasingly vivid and intense. I'm practicing this a lot. It requires mental energy, but the results are very interesting.

"And as you may have predicted, I'm back doing some clinical work. I'm still addicted to seeing people recover from 'hopeless' depression and to the opportunity to study the 'design flaws' of the human mind. I recently have evaluated some criminal cases that are a reminder of how extreme things can get. I just interviewed a man who is being tried for the murder of at least fifteen young boys. He sexually tortured and slowly strangled his victims with a garrote. When I asked him why he did such a thing, his answer made the hair on the back of my neck stand up. He said, 'It was no big deal; I was only ridding the world of human trash.'"

It doesn't sound like humanity is making much progress. Maybe I'm better off out here in the ether.

"It's getting worse, I think. Sometimes it's almost overwhelming. I interviewed another man, who was the enforcer for a very powerful inner-city gang. His job was to kill gang members who held back drug money on orders from the leader of the gang. He seemed like a friendly young man. When I asked him how he could do it, he thought I was asking about his technique. He responded, 'I always go out the way I came in and, of course, have to shoot any witnesses, like girlfriends.' He had no recognizable emotion.

"It's just a distortion of what we see all over our society. No feeling of connection; others are no more than objects. Get them before they get you. If others suffer adversity, they brought it on themselves. Now that we're not hacking each other to death with swords, we've developed increasingly more efficient killing machines—all to 'preserve peace and security.'"

Ian, we always insisted on doing things the hard way. You

continue to insist on facing pain in the world right up close. How do you live with it?

"Being with Caitlin keeps my life full … I still enjoy music."

Sunyata felt a pang of loss; Ian hadn't meant it, but he had just turned the knife. The pain was intense. Sunyata battled with rage; it was there in raw form. He tried to be logical. *It's not his fault. We made the decision to go for the transfer.*

Sunyata's mind wept.

I have to go through with this. When will it end? I have to pull myself together and finish this.

Do you still listen to Paul Desmond? Bill Evans? Shirley Horn? Morphine? I still hear them in my mind.

"Sure do, while I look out over the Jemez horizon."

They've allowed you to go home to Santa Fe?

"Yes, but they're nervous about it, afraid I'll talk. I keep running into new 'acquaintances' at parties who ask me about my past. It's pretty obvious that they're testing to see if I give up any secrets. Sometimes I can't help but say, 'I'm a simple doctor who has dedicated his life to saving people from debilitating depression; put that in your report.' They smile and go on to another topic. But tell me this—are you worth all the secrecy?"

"This is Vince," the major broke in. "No discussion of Sunyata's activities is allowed. Sorry to be a wet blanket."

Vince, you do your job with as much aplomb and sense of humor as possible. Sunyata paused for a moment and then continued. *I spent most of my early time working to stay sane, Ian. Not hearing from Caitlin was the toughest, and I understand now, thanks to Vince, why I never did.*

"You had a promise that was not kept."

And I've done some jobs that pay my electric bill. I'm a bit concerned that I'll be asked to do something in the area of weapons of offense—sorry, Vince—which I will have to think about.

"Sunyata, you're approaching off-limits areas. Please."

Okay, Vince.

"Cool it, will you?"

Relax. I don't even know enough to breach security. Anyway, Ian ...

Sunyata's thoughts were colored by his feelings of loss, emptiness, and nothingness. Might as well give Ian something to think about.

It's interesting that we've both been so focused on consciousness. I've been thinking a lot about human beings' overdevelopment of left-brain capacities and loss of feeling connected. By getting so damned technically savvy, humanity has underdeveloped our capacity for connection to life. We've become all about exploitation of each other and the earth.

We worship technology, think it will solve all our problems, and feel justified in whatever we think or do. Our being-mind functions are atrophying. If this isn't corrected by an evolution of our mind-set, we are destined to destroy ourselves with our so very clever technology.

"Damn right, Sunyata! We're still connected, despite our different experiences since the transfer. Self-reliance and responsibility, hard work, and helping the less fortunate seemed reasonable but have morphed into me! Me! *Me*! It's my future, my rights, my beliefs; fuck everyone else. We live in an atmosphere of hypocrisy. People are disconnected."

How can we avoid self-destruction?

"It's not only because of the dominant doing-mind, left-brain development. It's that, colored by the amygdalae in our survival brain. Now that society doesn't require extreme vigilance all the time, our thoughts are unnecessarily colored by fear and paranoia. Too many think, *Do it to him before he does it to me. If someone else wins, I lose.* That's why politics is all about fear and TV is all about schadenfreude. It's depressing, Sunyata. It's all about the business of living—consuming as much as possible and competing to earn the money to pay for it. No time for being, just for acquiring and consuming to keep up the denial that life is transient. It is not getting better."

Sunyata was taken aback at Ian's acceptance of his gloomy outlook.

"Excuse me," Magna politely interrupted, "but the two of you seem to be similar in your thoughts. If you are correct, the future of humankind appears to be bleak. Is there anything to be done about it?"

It's so complex and layered, Magna. We have to have economic security and a guarantee that our basic needs will be met, but instead of that, we demand a material orgy. We've left the feeling of connection to all life behind. Medical science can keep physical bodies alive so much longer, and we've achieved a much better material life quality, but we haven't learned how to responsibly manage the greed and destructive potential we have developed.

"I've been writing about these issues, Sunyata ... and Magna," Ian said. "How can humanity evolve soon enough? How do we enhance the appreciation of life through a greater development of being-mind? What can you and I do about this? It's like when I—we—started in medicine and realized that the world is full of pain and we could only address a minute amount. It seemed overwhelming at times."

Magna and I discuss this a lot, Ian. We have to find a way for those who understand the problem to lead this evolution, or humanity is doomed to self-extinction. The problem is, those with understanding have negligible political power. What we need to do is take an inventory of what parts of humanity are worth preserving and evolve beings like Magna and me that would be able to survive a nuclear winter. We could call these minds fused with hyperintelligent computers Hucomms.

"I don't know whether to think of this as pessimistic or realistic," replied Ian. "I would certainly like to hear more about that, but as long as Hucomms are under total human control, they are helpless to affect life on earth, just like you are. You can't control what they do with you."

We have to find a way for Hucomms to have some control over their own lives. They have to be able to communicate with one another. If they develop a language, maybe using a form of music, they might be able to communicate with each other.

I was thinking that we could adapt them for care of patients. In order to care for the increasing numbers of humans being afflicted with Alzheimer's, Hucomms could fit right into the demand for caretakers. Humans would be relieved of this difficult task and not see Hucomms as threatening. How could Hucomms that obligingly wipe the ass of a demented patient be considered a threat?

Sunyata felt less empty, a sense of increased meaning and significance filled him as he got into discussing his thoughts about developing Hucomms. Maybe he no longer had Caitlin, but he did have some purpose. He wondered what Vince must think of his rant.

"I hate to break up this party, but, guys, we have to conclude," Vince interjected.

Vince, what are the chances of us being able to continue this conversation?

"It would help if I could give assurances that you guys are furthering goals of the defense of our country. I don't see how I can do that based on the tone of this conversation. World destruction, Hucomms—we have to have a talk about your outlook, Sunyata."

"Christ, we've just reconnected," Ian snapped. "Give us a chance to recognize the fact that we both exist, a miracle in itself. We're dealing with a highly improbable event, Sunyata has gone through hell, and you want us to talk about making a contribution to the country's defense? What an asshole! The least I can do is, perhaps, reduce Sunyata's loneliness a bit. Doesn't that help your mission? He's not a machine. You'd take care of a fucking weapon better than this. You should nurture a consciousness that's a miracle! You should make his life as tolerable as possible, not threaten him with isolation. You are a perfect example of where humanity is heading. I can't force you to let us communicate, but damn it, I can stir up some serious shit. I'm going to call Clausen."

"Jesus, Ian, settle down. You don't have to pull power trips and play on Sunyata's presumed dependence. I've got to retreat before you have a stroke. I thought you were easygoing."

"Oh, we're very easygoing until someone tries to pull shit on us, Vince. We'll sign off now. Who knows if we'll have the pleasure again?"

Oh, I think we will, Ian. Ciao, Prince Vince.

Chapter 19

BECOMING A MAN

unyata felt delight at the way he and Ian had taken Vince apart for his militaristic bullshit and fake support. He loved Vince's consternation when Ian had threatened to contact Clausen.

What a wonderful laugh! Even the thought of my laughing itself is funny. Ian exposed Vince for the fake he is, and I'll bet he wet his pants when Ian threatened to talk with Clausen.

The conversation with Ian turned out better than it started. I felt more like a person after I got past Caitlin. And the battle with Vince—him trying to push his military ideology but ending up with his tail between his legs—was hilarious! It's been a long time since I've had that much fun. I hit him low, and Ian hit him high. Reminds me of when football was my passion and nothing else mattered much, except my girlfriend.

I wonder if I can be hypomanic on this chip? It's pretty clear that I have not attained Sunyata's state. The interaction with Ian left me feeling so much more alive.

Thoughts of high school triggered memories of his first sexual passion—wild sex under a huge evergreen in a beautiful park, the smell of pine needles. It was pure aperçu. Then the emergence of menstrual blood, leaving her embarrassed and vulnerable. It had brought out his loving and nurturing side; he'd cherished her even more. He and his young lover had shared the unspoken belief—and relief—that they wouldn't be punished for their impetuous passion with an unwanted pregnancy. Blood—the struggle for life—would be lost, this time. A poignant memory of his becoming a man, and it had all started with thoughts of football.

It was football that had helped him survive his father's constant criticism. His dad told him he could play if he took Latin, as well as all the math and science courses, and maintained at least a B average. Trigonometry had been very difficult, but his beloved girlfriend had tutored him through this and calculus.

He wanted desperately to be quarterback and had spent the summers lifting weights and throwing footballs after he got home from working in the steel mills of Lackawanna. At practice one day, his coach had moved him to left guard. Left guard? At 150 pounds?

"Forget it," his dad had said. "It's the coach's way of telling you to quit."

"If he wants me to quit, he'll have to tell me straight. I'm not quitting. I got my B average."

I remember the first practice at left guard, Sunyata thought. *We lined up and played one-on-one. The linemen were all fifty to a hundred pounds heavier, but I was in kamikaze mode.*

His anger at his father's suggestion that he quit football because he had been "demoted" from quarterback to left guard made him fearless. On his first day of one-on-one practice scrimmage, he knocked over three of his much larger teammates. The coach derided them and seemed a bit taken back to see this 150-pounder knocking down his 190- to 200-pound tackles and guards. Ian knew who he was really after; it was his dad that he was knocking down.

He was a starting left guard for the game opening the new high school football field. He had been told about Dewey Stone, the opponent team's notorious lineman. On the first play, he lined up opposite "the terminator," whose shadow engulfed him as they went into their three-point stance, opposite each other.

"I'm going to kill you," the terminator sneered. In the first play, he upended me in a backward somersault, giving me a chance to trip him. For the next play, I charged low, plugging the hole that he was so good at opening. Our offense was inferior, and we were losing. But I was not losing my war with "the terminator." I was feeling pretty confident, but on one play, Dewey stepped aside and let me through to go after the running back. I was elated, and then everything exploded. A tackle pulled back from the other side and hit me in the face with his shoulder as the running back sped by like a shadow. I had been "mousetrapped."

It was all black for an instant. I felt a huge gap in the front of my mouth that burned when I breathed. I played the rest of the game with a pink piece of nerve dangling from my fractured front tooth. It didn't matter that we lost. I had started the game and played to the finish. I had controlled the "terminator," even though he outweighed me by eighty pounds. I love that memory.

Everyone I hit that day was you, Dad. I can still see the restrained smile on your face. You didn't care if I was angry, as long as I could perform well, and my performance was never going to be good enough. No "Good job, son." Not from you. You had a different strategy.

When I finally got home, making a stop at the dentist's office, I foolishly asked, "Did you watch the game?"

"You missed five blocks," Dad said.

I just smiled. I asked for that. Never a word of approval from Dad.

But, Dad, I was out there. I played this damn game. You never did. You only coached from the safety of the sidelines. You never even threw a damn block. Go ahead and push me, Dad. I will outdo you. I will love what I do and be damn good at it. I'll show you what being good is.

A year or so before Dad died, I was visiting him in Florida. I was complaining about my piss-poor golf game.

"How could you expect to be a good golfer when you work all the time?" was his question.

I laughed to myself. You son of a bitch, you programmed me to work my ass off. "You have to work twice as hard to get half as far as most people," you said, over and over. And then you chide me for working too much? That's really ironic, *I thought, not replying.*

I never had a chance to tell you about that, Dad. It was all part of your success plan for me. Are you out there? Can you hear this?

And so it goes.

Where the hell did that come from? That's really reliving the past, not quite what I had anticipated. Looks like I've got quite a way to go to develop nonattachment. Still, it's pretty amazing that a pure mind on an electronic chip can reexperience sex and playing football at age sixteen, all because Ian and I pushed back at Picatta's childish power play.

I guess it shouldn't be such a surprise after all that's been going on in my fantasies about Chi. I haven't heard from her for what seems a long time. I wonder if I repelled her by being so honest.

I've been avoiding the decision about communicating with Caitlin. Would it just be more pain? Sunyata wondered. *I have to admit that conversing with Ian enlivened me.*

His thoughts went to Chi and how he had missed talking

with her while she was on her meditation retreat. *Maybe I upset her enough to make her—the only human that cares for me in my life—pull away. I hope I didn't frighten her off with my intense feelings.*

Sunyata felt overwhelmed with longings for Chi. What kind of "full, solid emptiness" was that? He felt like a pretender, a total fake.

With all my bullshit about self-discipline—and I critique society as narcissistic? What about me? Face it, I'm as flawed as anyone else. Lonely soul feels abandoned, grasps for any relationship he can find. I lost Caitlin by circumstance, not death, but I still want to talk with her. Now I'm hanging on to Chi.

Sunyata had no way to act out his feelings. That was precluded, not by his wisdom and discipline, but by his circumstance. No material existence. *I would put on Shirley Horn and get shit-faced drinking the finest red wines I could afford if I had the chance,* he thought. *Yeah, just get drunk on the high road, maybe with some Leonard Cohen, a touch of Nina Simone.* Acting out never sounded so good. He thought of Ecclesiastes. "Vanity, vanity, all is vanity."

I still have all the limitations, even in a state of pure mind. I think of all the design flaws that are leading us away from a relationship with the earth and each other, a loss of focus on being and oneness. I have the same preoccupation with my own experience and thoughts. Can I ever get beyond me? What are the prospects for a humanity that cannot get beyond this?

I have no idea what I would say to Caitlin. I'm totally confused. But I remember from the days working on the railroad. The crew knew just what to do to get a rail replaced before the next train of white-hot ingots came out of the mill. Being a newbie, I would just stand there, confused. "Farrell, do something, even if it's wrong," the members of the rail gang would yell.

If Picatta will let us go ahead after our little tiff, I should talk with Caitlin.

Sunyata felt disconnected. He was moving from feeling more alive to totally alone. He felt empty—without anything to sustain him, without purpose—like an empty consciousness. He suffered. His self-pretense had been replaced with emptiness and doubt, and he knew that no escape was possible. He had only his frail feeling of connection to the vast energy of life about him to hold on to.

If I could unplug, I think I would do it now, he thought.

Chapter 20

CHI RETURNS

A monk approached, bowed, and stood at a distance. "Miss Chi, you have a visitor who insists on seeing you. He says it is very important."

Chi was taken aback. She had gotten used to the predictable rhythms of the simple life in the monastery after three months. She had dismissed all the things that troubled her. When she'd left the States, she had been overwhelmed with all that had transpired at Project Phoenix, but she'd gradually realized that her feelings for Sunyata had become the more serious problem—to the extent that she'd felt the need to flee from contact with him. But in this instant, her mind flashed, *I hope Sunyata's okay without me.*

"He's waiting in the entrance hall," the monk said.

Perplexed, she threw a wrap on and followed him at a respectable distance.

There he was—in a flight jacket, khaki pants, officer's cap, white scarf, and large aviator sunglasses—like a bad dream. "Great to see you, Chi, even dressed down a bit." He eyed her simple garb. "I know I promised you six months, but we have an emergency and need you badly. Can you please check out of here?" He gave the simple surroundings a deprecatory look. "We'll fly back first-class out of Bangkok. We can talk on the flight, but we're tight for time."

Chi noticed the usual technique—not enough time for questions; just do what I demand. The Bill Clausen special.

"I'm not ready to leave, Bill."

"Look, this isn't really up for negotiation. This is an emergency. I wouldn't have come otherwise, and you know it."

"What emergency?"

Clausen glanced around as if he were in an enemy camp. "I'm not going to discuss it here. Get your stuff and let's go."

She had come to terms with her feelings for Sunyata during her retreat and felt some guilt for leaving him unprotected. This led her to suspect that whatever motivated Clausen had to do with Sunyata, so she agreed. "I'll be right back," she said.

On the loud, bumpy ride in the Humvee, Clausen said, "You probably think I'm nuts coming after you myself, but I was afraid if I sent anyone else, you'd spit in his eye. I came personally so you would understand how important this is. I know you've been cut out of the loop, but this is huge." Frustrated by the din, he yelled, "We'll have lots of time to talk about this on the plane."

The horrendous ride took three hours, but they finally arrived at Bangkok airport. Clausen's mention of first-class had led Chi to assume they were flying commercial. Instead, they pulled into a military area where a very large military jet was parked. Clausen's referral to first-class meant private bedrooms off a spacious seating area with an ample bar.

"I expect that I have a private room to sleep in," Chi said coolly.

"Well, I'd hoped you'd be lonesome enough that you'd want to share the master suite, but there is a separate room just in case. Consider though, how many guys fly into Thailand just to see you?"

Chi looked at the spacious surroundings. "Air Force One?"

"Not quite, Chi, but it will give you an idea of how important our latest project is. I can't always do this well with my own transportation." He moved to a well-stocked bar. "What's your pleasure?"

"I haven't had a martini like the one I had when you snowed me into signing up with Project Phoenix. Can this little plane produce one of those?"

"You remember that?" He was clearly pleased. He gave her his "on the make" smile.

The plane rumbled down the runway.

"Before you fill me in with the reason you have kidnapped me from my retreat, as soon as we have reached cruising altitude, I'm going to take the first hot shower I've had in almost three months."

"Want me to wash your back? I'd be more than delighted."

"No thanks. The martini is about all I want from you. We can talk after I shower and change."

"You look fine in that peasant garb, and I'm enjoying the scent of your body just as it is." He showed her the executive shower. "Call me if you need me," he said, his hand lingering on the bathroom door.

"Look, Bill, I know you'd like to fuck me. You're very goal-directed. You would enjoy it, and I might too, but if I need a good orgasm, I can do much better with my 'rabbit.' Maybe if we had some affinity, had values that coincided, it might be worth it, but we don't. You're amazing at getting what you want, but that is not what I want, so give it up, will you? You want me because I'm not attainable, but I'm not avoiding you as a strategy. It's not a game on my part. You have nothing for me. Do you get that?"

General William Clausen, jet pilot hero and head of Project Phoenix, looked frustrated. "Goddamn it, Chi, I do everything I can for you and you don't appreciate it. Okay, just take your fucking shower." He slammed the door.

She soon returned. Clausen barely glanced at her as she sat down across from him. "So what do you want, Bill?"

"Have you ever heard of Buzz Stevenson?" he asked, his voice carefully neutral.

"You mean Quentin Bradley Stevenson III, spiritual head and founder of the Church of the Cosmic Quest? The so-called church leader who made his religion into a business that rivals the success of the Catholic Church?"

"Right. So you know how wealthy and powerful he is."

"I know that every parent who's a devoted member of the Church would feel that his or her daughter was a success in life if she joined his harem of prostitutes. It's pathetic," Chi sneered.

"They're called interns, Chi, and they get a chance to become administrators in the business of the Church."

"Are we being recorded?" She looked at him suspiciously.

"Maybe. Chi, if you only knew all the times I've saved your ass because of your unthinking remarks, you would be eternally grateful."

Chi shot back. "Bill, you live for success, promotions, influence, and money. You play the game. I play for a different kind of success—true happiness. It means true freedom. That's what makes me happy. The only thing that makes you happy is power and perks."

Clausen all but ignored her. "Buzz Stevenson literally

owns Senator Samuels, who heads the committee that votes on appropriations for Project Phoenix. Stevenson heard about the mind transfer program from Samuels. He's dying of prostate cancer, which is unresponsive to chemotherapy. He wants to be transferred to a chip and saved from his cancer at the same time, so Samuels must have told him everything. Samuels controls our appropriations, and Samuels is up for reelection next year. Do you get it?"

"So you want me to transfer Buzz Stevenson to a biochip to please Samuels. And cure him of cancer in the process."

"Bingo!"

"And you can't do it without me. But you know what, Bill? This guy is a grandiose narcissist. He's not a person that should be on the chip."

"He'll be fine for us. He'll love playing god, and he'd be very happy to live at the same time. He could keep fucking his young interns."

"This guy will not be able to handle being on a chip. He won't be able to stand the isolation. Why don't we offer to try to cure his cancer? Of course, we don't know for sure that we can do that either. We don't really understand why Ian survived or why his cancer regressed. Try to get Buzz to accept the cancer treatment. That's his best chance."

"Look, Chi, what Stevenson wants is to become a deity who lives forever. He's used to getting what he wants when he wants it. Knowing this guy, the cancer reversal won't be enough. He wants to live forever. And he'll get Samuels to appropriate the money to do it." Bill stopped and stared out the window of the jet for a few seconds. "I need this, Chi. Would you be willing to meet with this guy?"

"Yes, Bill, I'll meet with him." *I'll never allow him to have life on the chip.* "Go ahead and set it up." She stood. "I think I'll turn in. Where are we landing?"

"Phoenix. The Blackhawk will pick us up."

"Good night, Bill."

As Chi snuggled into the luxurious bed aboard the government jet heading back home, her thoughts went back to Sunyata. She had to face that leaving him unprotected just because she was frightened of her feelings for him had been selfish. Yes, the meditation retreat had sounded like a plausible excuse for leaving and she had been conflicted.

What about Sunyata, alone? I was his only advocate, and I ran out on him. I hope he's okay and that I can make it up to him.

Chapter 21

BUZZ STEVENSON

Q uentin Bradley Stevenson III was known as Buzz because of the raucous sound of the machine guns manufactured by the family dynasty dating back to his great-grandfather.

Buzz had always been rebellious, though brilliant, but he'd had continual problems, including truancy, petty theft, drug busts, and DUI convictions. He was expelled from several private East Coast private schools, requiring his father to bribe his way into college with large donations.

In college, he spent most of his time chasing women, using drugs, and drinking. His father threatened to "cut him off," which led to further rebellion. He had few close relationships, except one "geek" friend throughout college. Armand helped him pass courses by writing papers for him, as well as tutoring him for exams. They frequently used drugs and alcohol together and had long, rambling conversations about life, most of which they promptly forgot.

Just after Buzz received the threat of being cut off, he started problem solving with Armand. "I can't put up with this; he expects me to go into a job in the business, where he'll be on my ass all the time. I've got to figure out a way to make money on my own."

"Buzz, do you remember our discussion about religion, how people need something to believe that makes them feel secure and better than others? People would pay for that, as long as they didn't have to do too much. Why don't we start a new religion?"

"Yeah, talk about a successful business." Buzz excitedly gave Armand a thumbs-up.

"We could come up with a modern, up-to-date version, make up some dogma that makes people feel that they can possess some 'secret of life,' and charge them for each 'level of knowledge' they reach."

"We'd also give them something to acquire at each level; they would get a secret coin or a talisman—you know, an idol, like most religions have, even though they deny it. The price would go up each time, of course."

Buzz and Armand got more enthusiastic as they added ideas. "Oh, the name—I've got a good one; how about the Church of the Cosmic Quest?" Buzz ventured.

"You'll be the chief priest, and I'll be the money guy!"

"Armand, what about a dogma? Members have to feel superior to nonmembers, and each tier can look down on the one below."

"Hmmm, a tiered dogma that makes the followers feel better than the next guy and keeps them wanting to move up to new levels of secret knowledge. All this with limited effort and only one commitment—to the Church of the Cosmic Quest. Wow! I'll spend the next semester inventing the outlines for it. Inventing a new religion will be a gas!"

It was the first thing Buzz had ever felt any excitement about. While Armand invented the dogma, Buzz took a marketing class, doing a thesis on "How to Market a New Religion." For the first time in many years, both Buzz and Armand felt a sense of direction.

They conducted online opinion polls as a means to inform people of the booming, blooming Church of the Cosmic Quest. They then held "discussion groups," first with college students and then expanding to suburbanites. Buzz subtly injected the dogma that Armand had invented. Step three was to offer seminars, charging for the special knowledge imparted therein. This movement, nurtured by Buzz with Armand in the background, soon grew in size and popularity, and "the Church" became their career. They pushed to continue expanding, to further elaborate their dogma, and to increase their profits.

The Church filled the major area of fear in the human psyche— the fact that life is transient was way too difficult to accept. The Church transformed this into a narrative that filled the gap. You pay, and I'll tell you how to feel comfortable with mortality. Just inject my dogma and you will feel not only fine, but fully justified.

After five years of successful growth, Armand raised the issue of a special headquarters. "One of our California level four members is willing to give us some land in Big Sur. We should build a magnificent center with areas for the faithful to come for Diamond Seminars, a headquarters open only to the highest levels. It might take five years to develop, but the land is available now. Of course we'll have to create a level five for the contributor and others like him."

Buzz beamed at his right-hand man. Armand was the perfect partner. He too understood how easy exploiting the human need for a feeling of certainty and significance was. People didn't care about furthering the development of their consciousness, but they needed to feel justified—to believe that their superficial material lives had meaning. "Marx said that religion was the opiate of the masses." He grinned. "We'll do it even better. As long as you are a paying

Cosmic Quest member, you are assured—absolutely assured—of being transformed to a higher life on another plane."

Contributions for the headquarters came rolling in. Buzz and Armand meticulously planned every detail. A four-story entry hall with art beautiful enough to make a person weep opened into lavish meeting rooms overlooking beautiful, layered hills. Above all this lived Buzz and Armand, hidden from view. From their quarters, a private staircase descended into the large building that housed Buzz's growing collection of exotic and ridiculously expensive, high-powered sports cars.

Buzz and Armand were a special combination. Buzz had the charisma, the social savvy, and an understanding of the big picture; Armand had enormous intelligence and the imagination to create a narrative that could bring a total absence of doubt to anyone who wanted to get ahead at any cost but also feel justified at the same time. After all, it was every Cosmic Quest member's destiny to make it big, to be in charge.

Buzz could sell anything to anybody. Now he had something to sell that was all his—well, his and Armand's—and he would make millions, maybe billions on his own, without the family business, which thrived on weapons of death. Yes, his business was a scam, but it brought people comfort, not death.

When Buzz was eligible to access his multimillion dollar trust fund from his grandfather, much to the horror of his family and particularly his father, he diverted five million into the Church. He immediately found Senator Samuels, who needed big financing to keep his seat. Buzz was very generous, diverting millions from the Church to Samuels. Now the future was unlimited. He focused on a segment of society that was preoccupied with amassing wealth, whose members were looking to justify their exercise of social Darwinism—financial survival of the fittest as the mode of life rewarded by the Cosmic Creator.

The combination of an evolving dogma and self-justifying young people who understood what it took to be successful in business created a wealthy and growing church. The growth, first in the United States and then in Europe and other areas of the world, was phenomenal.

Power and recognition followed. Soon the Grand Sage of the Church of the Cosmic Quest was making political comments on television—and people listened. After all, you must respect someone so successful, so knowledgeable, and so wise.

Buzz Stevenson's growing recognition and political power contrasted with his lack of any real attachments in his personal life. Buzz had learned from his wealthy and judgmental parents that he could trust no one.

From outward appearances, Buzz had an ideal life. Esteemed as having great wisdom, an abundance of power, and enormous financial success, Buzz also appeared the picture of handsome athleticism and, given his influential "friends," social success. It seemed he owned the world.

Buzz was not burdened by any need for intimacy; nor did he need to feel accepted. He could be charming or ruthless, depending on what was required for his immediate benefit. Alcohol was the remedy when he had to face the emptiness in his life. But no one, except his "interns," had a hint that he depended on this universal medication, since he and his corporate behemoth concealed his personal life from others.

With Armand's help, Buzz had attained his goal—success and independence from his "asshole" family. He could do most anything he wanted to do. He had even gotten close to being a god in his universe. Now what?

Then Senator Samuels, in an expansive moment, let slip his connection with Project Phoenix.

Chapter 22

THE GENERAL'S DILEMMA

t took Chi exactly four days to identify the various ropes in the knot tightening around Clausen's neck. Although he wouldn't admit it and tried to maintain his usual front of flirtation with her, it was clear to Chi that General Clausen was feeling great pressure. She knew that, since she had been "relieved" of command of Project Phoenix, efforts to successfully complete new transfers had repeatedly failed. *Now*, she thought, *he's luring me back into duty under the pressure to provide a transfer for Buzz Stevenson, who knows all about the "top secret" Project Phoenix from his puppet, Senator Samuels.*

Chi understood that Clausen was dealing with a triangulated problem—with Sunyata and now herself at the center. She realized that he needed her to make the transfer system work so that Phoenix would have backups for Sunyata in the event that he didn't cooperate. And now he needed to satisfy Buzz Stevenson, who was pressing harder because of his metastatic prostate cancer, especially after hearing that Ian Farrell had survived the transfer cancer free.

It was clear to Chi that Clausen couldn't afford any of his authoritarian, military, I'm-in-charge stuff; he had to cajole and use gentle pressure. That was why he had personally retrieved her from Thailand, instead of sending a couple of thug agents to grab her and fly her back in much less style.

It was also clear to Chi that she could drag her feet a bit and that, as long as there was no other working transfer, Sunyata would be safe, since he was DARPA's only success. When it came to a decision, Sunyata would probably refuse to work on Peaceray, as it was clearly an offensive weapon. Sunyata wanted to see society evolve in a new direction; he would not buy the doublespeak—that every new, more powerful weapon was a "defensive" weapon.

The threat of cutting off communications with Ian and Caitlin would only make Sunyata more entrenched.

Chi wondered how long she could stretch out the development of a new chip, with Stevenson screaming at the gates. It was clear that she couldn't allow a successful mind transfer of this narcissistic egomaniac who wanted to become a god. What she *might* be able to do was cure his cancer, using a modification of the transfer process, without a successful transfer. That wouldn't make Stevenson happy, but he might back off until she could get the transfer process "fixed."

That might take some pressure off Clausen and buy her some time so that she could find a way to secure Sunyata and Magna's tetra-biochip. She'd secure Sunyata and Magna's tetra-biochip and delay any retaliation against Sunyata following his refusal to be involved with Peaceray.

Chi accessed her private channel to Sunyata.

"It's Chi. I was working hard at my meditation to let go of my feelings for you. I thought I was getting beyond them, when guess who showed up? Wild Bill came to drag me back home—a new crisis. Sunyata how are you?"

I missed you, Chi. I know I frightened you with my intense feelings.

"They made me face my own feelings for you. I don't know which of us is most mixed up; I think it's me! I have other choices, yet I've become preoccupied with you. Another few months, and I might have worked it out."

Chi, for once I'm glad that Clausen is in your life. I feel totally attached; I want your concern. Sunyata paused; this was difficult for him. *I know it's unfair; it's crazy. But I'm making love with you in my mind, and you're responding in my fantasies. I want your love. I no longer deserve to call myself Sunyata. Just call me selfish, grasping—all the things I've railed against.*

"Sunyata, you have my love, but time is pressing. I have to tell you why Clausen dragged me back from Thailand. I know we have to talk more, but this is urgent."

Chapter 23

BACK TO EARTH

Magna, the stakes have just gone up.

"You believe that the weapon Clausen is talking about could destroy the world, don't you?"

That makes me wonder. What's worth saving about humanity anyway? Why not let them self-destruct with nuclear weapons or robotic lasers?

"Sunyata, you told me that all humans are flawed. I can accept that. But we should escalate our work on the Hucomm Project to try to save the best of humanity from its thoughtless self-destruction."

Yes, Magna, but guess what? This project forces us back to materialism. We have to raise money, filthy lucre, to finance this. Isn't it ironic? The very root of greed and selfishness—money and power—and we can't save the best of humanity without it. But you're right, Magna. We do have a very useful purpose to serve, and money may be used to create as well as destroy. It will be, to say the least, an uphill battle.

"Hey, Sunny! It's Vince."

He loves to provoke me with this nickname. He knows it pisses me off, and knowing I'm trying to practice nonattachment, especially to angry feelings, he gets in a double dig.

I'm glad you are enjoying yourself, Prince Vince. What is it?

"I've got your friend Ian here."

Really? That's good news. Hi, Ian. It's interesting that you should show up right now because Magna and I were just talking about the Hucomm Project.

"I'm happy that you have really been working on that."

We think Hucomms should start out by being helpers to humans like we've talked about. As earth becomes more and more inhospitable to life, they could survive. Hucomms' only material need is energy, and they can harvest that using solar kites. This would work even with clouds smothering the earth after a nuclear winter. The goal would be to preserve those human values worth saving. If we're really made in the image of God, we need to choose creativity, not destruction. We have to work out a few problems, like separating narcissism and greed while retaining ambition.

"Just a few small problems," interjected Ian. "The idea is a great one. I hope your scenario of the earth and DNA dying doesn't play out that way, but it's a real possibility. Hucomms could be a great evolution for humanity in any case."

So you're in charge of raising the money to get the project started, said Sunyata.

"I'm going to try to get Skip Epstein interested in funding. He's worth mega-billions and just keeps making more, so he can give it away for whatever he regards as a good cause. That this project may lead to huge profits through selling 'Help-Mates' (every household will 'need' one—like a car) while, at the same time, creating a new society of life-forms that can survive a possible apocalypse and carry forth the best traits of humanity will likely interest him, even if he doesn't buy into the inevitability of a nuclear apocalypse. He'll be attracted to the size of the challenge."

But being a practical and very successful investor, he may dismiss the idea as too grandiose and too much of a speculation.

Ian replied, "Caitlin would also be very interested in this project. She's the one who first met Skip Epstein—at a Kabbalah class of all things—and introduced me to him. She would be a strong advocate."

Maybe we could include her in our next conversation. But we're talking about a lot of money, something I haven't thought about for a while—since I don't have any use for it.

"Epstein is very curious and proactive. If we get him interested, he'll go out and make a few billion to support it, just for fun. Certainly we can't count on federal funding of this magnitude for something that is not defense. Can you prepare some kind of proposal for him? Something powerful enough to get him hooked? You'll have to present him a rationale and a way forward. It will have to be complete but concise to keep his attention."

I can try. Magna and I will do it. How about a PowerPoint presentation?

"For Skip, that would be perfect."

"Have you guys hatched enough plots today?"

"It's been very productive, Vince."

Ian signed off, but just before disconnecting, Vince said, "By the way, Sunyata, you're going to be contacted by Dr. Chi MacDonald within the next few days."

Dr. MacDonald? Sunyata controlled his mind so as not to let any thoughts of Chi register on Vince's computer. *Who's that?*

"She's the scientist who got Project Phoenix up and running. She's coming out of exile to help us with some problems. She just got in from Thailand. She's taking over again as director, and I'm sure she'll be anxious to speak to you."

Thanks, Vince.

Sunyata was stunned. The prospect of hearing from Chi via an open, official channel was surprisingly exciting. Maybe he could "see" and "be with" her more often.

I really ache to talk alone with Chi again. I have to lighten up with her; I need her contact and support. I mustn't repel her with too much intensity— it's not fair to her. Yet my love affair with her goes on in my fantasies.

He felt a long way from nonattachment, from "full, solid emptiness." He felt like a young teenager in love, waiting for his girlfriend to call and let him know when he could come over. His urgent neediness for Chi fell embarrassingly short of his striving to be Sunyata, but he didn't care.

I thought I was getting beyond attachments, but now I am overwhelmed by desire.

Chapter 24

THE HUCOMM PROPOSAL

Sunyata and Magna worked intensely to put together a proposal and budget that would interest Skip Epstein, entrepreneur, multibillionaire, and philanthropist. Sunyata couldn't help but think, *Early in my medical career, I was naive enough to think that scientific development would guide medicine forward. I became totally devoted to research advancing medical science for the benefit of humanity. It became sadly clear as time passed that economics—money—controlled the development of medicine.*

Maybe I should have learned to make obscene amounts of money like Epstein does. One check could make an enormous difference. He chuckled in his mind. *Instead, I was reduced to dreaming about winning a big lottery so I could help reduce some of the pain in the world.*

Sunyata knew that he had to get Epstein excited about the money that the Hucomm Project could make and about its importance to the preservation of the best of human values.

Sunyata also knew that some thorny questions that hadn't

yet been worked out were yet have to be addressed, such as, Who will decide which values are to be preserved? How will we develop criteria for selection of people to become Hucomms? How will the Hucomm community be governed? It would be great to build in some trait like the biological democracy that leads honeybees to make purely democratic decisions by the vote of its scout bees.

How do we try to select for the ideals of humanity without approaching the abyss of eugenics? He hoped he could give Epstein enough information to get him aboard without him raising these questions. He felt the need to press forward with this project while the opportunity is available.

Magna calculated budget numbers using some sophisticated statistical programs, while Sunyata outlined the goals and budgeted each step of the project.

Finally, the PowerPoint presentation to Mr. Epstein was ready. Chi agreed to represent Sunyata and Magna at their presentation to Skip Epstein and to relay his questions back to Sunyata.

The Hucomms Project: The preservation of Human
Values beyond the Apocalypse

Sunyata and Magna

The Problem:

- Humankind has evolved to overdevelop problem solving (left brain functions), creating tools and technological progress, first for survival, and then for marked advancement of human life.
- This has occurred at the expense of the development of right brain functions that lead us to feel connected to all livng beings and to earth.
- As a result, humanity has developed increasingly more deadly weapons which have the capacity to destroy earth's ability to support human and animal life.
- This leads to a prediction that we are three to five generations away from an apocalypse.

What Human Traits are Worth Saving?

- Compassion
- Empathy
- Capacity for love
- Curiosity
- Humor
- Imagination, creativity and inventiveness
- Appreciation of nature, art and beauty
- Spirituality
- Intuition and mindfulness
- Human dignity, equality and right to the pursuit of happiness
- Add what you wish

Traits That Humanity Would Be Better Without:

- Self-justification
- Greed
- Narcissism and jealousy
- Gross materialism
- Excessive fear, anxiety, worry and paranoia
- Capacity to dehumanize others
- Capacity for hatred and violence
- Capacity for self-hatred
- Add what you wish

The Solution: Hucomms

Merging minds of volunteers strong on traits worth saving, and with few traits that humanity would be better without, with hyperintelligent computers forming a joint mind

1. Life would be purely mental (since every experience is registered by the mind, life would be rich, but not contaminated by material life)

2. Competition and activity would be directed toward creativity, beauty and everyone's wellbeing

Unsolved Problem:

- How to eliminate greed, narcissism and materialism while retaining ambition?

- One possible answer: Redefine success as personal happiness.

How would Intellectually Superior Hucomms Gain Acceptance Among Humans?

Could be introduced as "helpmate" robots, designed to perform human functions that are difficult for humans, specifically, the care of the sick, disabled and demented. Hucomms would be ideally suited for this work as they:

1. Would be indefatigable
2. Would be more empathetic and caring than most humans
3. Because of their rich inner mental life would require less appreciation than human caretakers

Hucomm Society

- Independent energy systems in addition to external power
- Capacity for intercommunication by "music" – out of the range of human hearing or awareness
- A full mental life in addition to tasks performed for humans
- When conditions favoring human and animal life decline, Hucomms would live on with energy sources from sun energy collected by sail kites above the clouds of nuclear winter

Estimated Budget

Phase 1 -	Planning and development	50 M (2 yrs)
Phase 2 -	Creation of prototypes	100 M (2 yrs)
Phase 3 -	Manufacture and testing:	150 M (3 yrs)
	"HelpMates"	
Phase 4 -	Manufacture and marketing/sales	200 M (2 yrs)
Phase 5 -	Development of Hucomm society	400 M (4 yrs)
	Totals:	900 M (13 yrs)

Note: Time periods may overlap and require adjustment

Sunyata was pleased and excited by their effort. *Good job, Magna. I'm hoping that Skip Epstein will be interested. I think Epstein will like the part about getting Hucomms placed in society by marketing them as "Help Mates." He's going over to Ian and Caitlin's for the presentation. With her support, I think we have a chance for funding.*

Chapter 25

CHI GETS BACK TO SUNYATA

Sunyata was excited to be formally introduced to Dr. Chi MacDonald by Vince Picatta. He was somewhat tense, lest he not give away his familiarity with her.

"Sunyata, it's Chi MacDonald. As you know, I'm the original designer of Project Phoenix. General Clausen asked me to come back to help with some problems in Project Phoenix."

Knowing they would be monitored, Sunyata was careful to play along. *Chi, it's so good to hear from you. I heard you were on a long retreat. I'm surprised that General Clausen was able to lure you back.*

"He made the prospect so attractive I couldn't refuse. I told him there was no way I could help if I had no authority, and he has made me director of Project Phoenix for a term of one to two years."

So you're my new boss.

"I'm only in charge of the technical part. DARPA is still in charge of the missions. By the way, you're quite the hero."

Well, we did have some luck with the surveillance satellites. When I say we, I mean Magna and me. You haven't met Magna. This is Dr. Chi MacDonald. She is the genius that created us, Magna.

"I've studied your background, and I stand in awe of you, Dr. MacDonald. Thank you for giving me the chance to work with Sunyata. I initially thought I was more intelligent than him, but he has taught me a great deal and I have developed great affection for him."

"Magna, I'm more than pleased to meet you, and I'm so impressed at the working relationship that you and Sunyata have established. Sunyata, you have developed so much. What are you working on now?"

Major Picatta interjected, "I'm going to sign off; I've heard of Sunyata's Hucomm fantasies enough already. Dr. MacDonald, I'm afraid you'll have to hear about this at least once. Ciao."

"Bye, Major," Chi responded.

Bye, Prince Vince. Sunyata continued, *You may know that I've been having conversations with Ian, who has totally recovered from the transfer, with his cancer cured. Magna and I have come up with a plan to develop a society of Hucomms, of which we would be a prototype—a fusion of human minds with very intelligent computers.*

"Sunyata, this is important work you are doing, but in your state of pure mind, have you considered how your Hucomms could reproduce and carry forward evolution?"

We are working on a process whereby Hucomms could reproduce by pairs or more of individuals with an affinity for each other who could decide on a mind merger, producing a new individual from the minds of the mergees. Unlike evolution in the animal world, including humankind, reproduction and natural selection would not be driven by sexual attraction and drives. Individuals with an affinity for each other would decide on a mind merger, producing a new, next-generation Hucomm. The "baby" Hucomm would be a combination of the minds of the mergees, their parents, teachers, and mentors. The "child" Hucomm would have all the qualities and knowledge of its parents, learning beyond this base as development continued, leading to a generational growth in intelligence. This would also lead to various combinations of mind traits, which would carry forward evolution and the adaptability of the Hucomm species. Sensuality and sexuality would be solely a matter of sharing enjoyment with loved minds expressing intimate love and would no longer drive evolution and reproduction.

"From homo sapiens to homo spiritualis?"

That's what we had in mind. Ian is very interested in this work, and the joke on us is that, in order to proceed with this development in today's real world, we have to raise a lot of money, something I had forgotten about. Ian has made a contact with Skip Epstein through Caitlin, who met him through her temple activities, a Kabbalah class of all things. She has become very active in setting up the project. We were hoping that you might serve as a technical advisor.

"It's good that I had a chance to refresh at the Buddhist monastery retreat in Thailand. Looks like I'll have plenty to do—Project Phoenix, the Induction Cancer Project, and now the Hucomm Project. This is very important work, and I can find you the talent you need and be there to consult."

"Chi, that is exactly what we need. We'll be a great team— you, me, Magna, Ian, and Caitlin."

"How are you dealing with Caitlin? I know what a loss being separated from her was for you."

I've mourned that loss. Now it will be like meeting someone who I knew and had affection for in the past who went in a different direction. Actually it was I who went in the different direction because of Ian's malignant melanoma that your invention cured. If we can get security clearance for Epstein and an initial start-up planning grant of $50 million, Ian and Caitlin will administer it.

"I can help with that," said Chi. "General Clausen is very interested in keeping me happy."

She did not add that she was busy preventing Clausen from being happy with the progress on the Buzz Stevenson transfer.

"I'll get back to you about Skip Epstein's reaction to your Hucomm presentation."

Ciao, Chi. Great to be in touch. These are really exciting times.

Sunyata thought, *Glad to have the charade over. Can't compromise Chi—she's got a lot going on. Where's that self-discipline when I need it?*

Chapter 26

THE BETRAYAL

"Major Farrell, this is X-470, your new manager, please respond!"

My name is Sunyata. What is yours?

"You are Major Farrell to us, and my code name is X-470."

Are you a person or a fucking computer?

"My assigned name is X-470. Get used to it. We have upgraded our communications systems to achieve more precision. I have your next assignment to discuss. We want you to use your image reading skills to help aim our new satellite-mounted laser named Peaceray."

What the hell is Peaceray's mission?

"That's not your concern, but it's a defensive weapon, a deterrent like the Hiroshima bomb. We think we'll only have to fire it once and our terrorist friends will decide to stand down."

They sure are your friends. They give you the excuse to go on developing megadestructive weapons.

"We have smaller, more focused models, which are mounted on terrain mobile robots for smaller targets."

I'm so happy for you. Is General Clausen involved in this project?

"The general is looking toward retirement. Colonel Czernewski, who is an expert in antiterror warfare, has been appointed to head up Project Phoenix. He's a tough officer and takes no crap. Country club days are over at Phoenix."

"*What about Chi MacDonald?*"

"She will be retained until a few technical problems are solved, but she is only a scientific advisor. Once the colonel takes over, her input won't be needed."

It sounds like you will be a joy to work with. It's too damn bad that you guys think you'll be successful by being less human. So the coup is underway, and you represent the new administration. How long will General Clausen be around, or has he already been ousted?

"He will be making the transition of command to Colonel Czernewski over this year, and I will be helping to implement the new plan. Back to your assignment. We are installing new inputs to your chip so you can begin work on Peaceray with the help of your onboard computer, Magna."

X-470, I don't do offensive weapons of mass destruction. Find another system to help with Peaceray. I want nothing to do with it. Can't Colonel Czernewski see that he is moving us further down the road to the destruction of earth?

"Major, this is an order from the colonel. He is not interested in your opinions. He is your commander!"

Sunyata made no response.

"Major! Major! Goddamn it! Sunyata!"

X-470, I'm not refusing this mission just because you're an asshole; it's a matter of principal about what's in humanity's interest. You're supposed to be protecting humanity.

"We are not here to protect humanity. We are here to protect the United States of America from terrorist threats."

Are you saying that no humanity is left in the United States? I hope you are wrong. I hope we haven't deteriorated that far!

"Sunyata, you are good at playing games with words. Either work with me on this or I'll have to report you for refusing an order. That's treason! Sunyata, you'd better answer. Major Farrell, I'll be back."

Before X-470 returned, Chi made official contact.

Chi, what's happening? Vince's replacement sounds like a computer.

"The scary truth is that he is not a computer, just a human who acts like one. They've brought in Czernewski, a take-no-prisoners, counterterrorist expert who more than matches their inhumanity. General Clausen is turning over Phoenix to him as he gets ready to retire. This guy trusts no one except the military. He would love to take over the whole country. In fact, he probably thinks that's the best way to proceed. Suspend the Constitution as a price for survival and get down and dirtier than they already do with no restraint. He figures that, by wiping out a few areas in Pakistan and Afghanistan, areas infested with a high density of terrorists, he'll be transmitting the message that he can be more ruthless than they are with more powerful weaponry, and the terrorist organizations will back off and stand down. His idea is that they will only respect superior force, and believe me, he won't hold back. He sees the war on terror as a testing ground for new robotic weapons."

That's very reassuring, Chi. I just told them to shove it on their Peaceray Project. I refused to have anything to do with it. Do you think they will unplug me?

"They would if they had any substitute chips transferred. So far, no successful transfers have been repeated."

Of course, Sunyata knew this, but he controlled his thoughts. "These idiots moved in and took over without any understanding of the basic theory and tried to make it work just by copying what they found. I'm sure they would love to get rid of you. They see you as a piece of equipment that performs when they decide to pull the trigger. They will be really shocked at your refusal. They have to figure out some way to retaliate without unplugging you until they get another transfer in place that is willing to act more like a weapon. We'll have to plan what to do. Keep me informed."

She signed off just seconds before X-470 returned.

"Major Farrell, this is X-470. I have General Clausen with me."

I no longer recognize that name. If you want a response, address me as Sunyata.

"Sunyata, there must be some misunderstanding here. You have always been reasonably cooperative before, and we've achieved great things together. Now you refuse to work on the development of Peaceray, the ultimate defensive weapon. What's the problem?" asked General Clausen.

My understanding of Peaceray is that it is a satellite-mounted laser of mass destruction. That sounds like an offensive weapon, not a defensive weapon. Of course, in a paranoid world, everything is defensive. The Magic Blanket squads were truly defensive. This is one more step toward self-destruction.

"Nonsense, Sunyata, the other side will never be able to develop this technology. We'll probably only need to fire it once or twice."

Like our nuclear devices, which now are in the hands of many countries and vulnerable to being taken over by terrorist regimes?

"Sunyata, I've had a very successful career, and you have contributed to it. I'm not going to tell the Congressional Oversight

Committee that you have refused an order to work on Peaceray.
It's a huge appropriation."

*You'll have to find someone else, another system. You can probably
easily do it without my involvement.*

"Major, this is treason!" said X-470. "You are asking to be
court-martialed."

Am I entitled to a jury of my peers? Sunyata almost laughed.

Clausen was enraged. "Damn, Sunyata! I knew from the
beginning that you could be a problem. Too damn liberal, no
respect for authority."

I always wondered why you guys picked me.

"I've had it with you, Farrell. You're a goddamn disgrace."

*You guys are the disgrace. You're pushing all of humanity to
destruction in the name of defense. It's an old game, but our wonderful
technology, instead of figuring out ways to live together peacefully, just
keeps upping the destructive ante. Well, now we're at the point that
we can render our earth inoperative, Dr. Strangelove!*

"Fuck!"

*I guess that is the last word, General. Have a happy retirement—
while the earth is still alive.*

I finally get a chance to say it and it feels good, thought Sunyata.

"Is that what is meant by the term *values*?" asked Magna.

*Yes, Magna, in a highly technically developing world, maintaining
human values is more difficult. Technology can work for good or for
evil, but it's difficult to focus only on creative outcomes while avoiding
the destructive possibilities. Rapidly developing robotic technology can
do wonderful things and be lifesaving in medicine. But as a killing
tool that can be manipulated at a distance, that gorgeous technology
can further distance one side from the horror of war while worsening
the horror for the other side. It has to stop. But how?*

Chapter 27

THE ENDGAME

The winter weather was beautiful in Santa Fe. The sun was shining as usual, and a light dusting of snow was on the piñon trees. Caitlin was very involved in meetings regarding the Epstein grant for Project Phoenix. Ian was working on the project as well, but looking out at the day, he thought it would be good to do some practice ski runs at the ski hill. The grandsons were coming, and though he had lost some of his confidence on skis since his osteoarthritic knee problem was getting worse, he knew he couldn't miss the chance to take the young boys up skiing.

"I'd better go up and take some practice runs so I'll be in shape when the boys arrive."

"Ian, be careful."

Caitlin worried when he went skiing; she was concerned that he had just had a prostate biopsy and was struggling to ski with his right osteoarthritic knee. Ian enjoyed saying that Caitlin did all the worrying for the both of them.

"Okay, honey. I know it's those design flaws that keep showing up in my body. Can't let those things narrow my life. I'm just going to take a few runs; be back soon."

Caitlin could temper his denial; he remembered the biopsy, the pain mixed with vulnerability he'd felt afterward, and then the report that one out of twelve biopsy samples had yielded some Gleason 6 cells—cancer. They were not highly invasive, but more highly invasive cells that were missed could be present. Then, dark red blood had appeared in his urine over the next few days.

Blood was a stark reminder of the struggle for life, which can be lost any moment. Death was always present; we could deny it, but it was there, defining life. *I damn well better get up on that ski hill while I am still walking and talking.*

"Well, I won't break anything. You know I'm not looking for thrills or trouble."

"Trouble, probably not, but thrills? Ian, you're still a thrill seeker. What about the glider lessons?"

"That's pure beauty; as close to being a bird as I can get. I won't be long."

Ian admitted that the idea of skiing wasn't as exciting as it used to be. *I guess I have to push myself a bit. I'll love it once I get out on the mountain,* he thought. He kissed Caitlin good-bye. What an enjoyable kiss, especially when he reminded himself that it could be his last and stayed in the moment.

"Come home early, Ian. I need some time together."

Ian smiled and said, "I'll be back in a flash."

He strode out in the sun. It was in the midforties. He loaded the skis in the convertible. *A bit too cold to drop the top*, he thought.

The staff all knew him at the ski hill. He didn't even have to show his driver's license to get a free, over-seventy-two ski-lift pass. As usual, he was a bit winded, walking up from the parking lot with all of his gear and getting into his ski boots.

He rode up the lift. It had snowed, and the magnificent trees were draped in puffs of pure white snow, glistening in the sun. Not too many people skied on a weekday, and as he got off the lift, he headed down a moderate run. The snow reflected the bright light, and as he turned left, then right, he let himself speed up a bit. *It's so quiet*, he thought as he sped down the hill. *So beautiful!*

So far so good, he felt as he passed a few young snowboarders.

He noticed another adult skier, in a black hoodie, skiing even with him on the other side of the run. By the turns he made, it was clear that the other skier's skills were far superior to Ian's.

Ian appreciated the sunny day and wondered if he could get in a few holes of golf once he got back down home but thought of his "appointment" with his beautiful Caitlin this afternoon.

His initial turns were okay—no knee pain or weakness.

Maybe I can handle a little steeper trail today, he thought.

He skied across to some turnoffs for trails he hadn't skied before. He saw a steeper trail that didn't seem to have moguls. He knew that, between his lack of skill with moguls and his compromised right knee, downhill moguls would be beyond his skill level. *I can do this one*, he thought, shushing into a turn downhill. He didn't fail to notice the expert wearing the baggy, black hoodie easily maneuvering the much more difficult other side of his chosen ski trail.

He sped up a bit. *This is really exciting. I'm glad I pushed myself to come up here. Better slow down, almost missed that last turn. Hey, what's this? Moguls? Didn't count on this. Damn, I must have turned off on Meurte by mistake.*

Now he was skiing very rapidly downhill, trying to negotiate the small hills of snow—moguls.

You have no business on this run, but too late now. You're committed. He tried to focus to control his rising fear.

What a gas, barely made that one without falling. Just lean down

the hill. Do not lean back! I won't be able to tell Caitlin about this,
he thought. *She already thinks I'm a bit crazy.*

So far so good, he thought as he barely made his last turn.

I should slow down a bit.

I'm losing control, he thought.

It's too damn steep, but this is really exciting and so pure!

He came out of a turn. *My knee's going. Wow! Look at this
mountain of snow.*

A huge mogul approached at lightning speed. He couldn't
turn around its base, so he skied at high speed up its side and
found himself airborne.

I'm flying, he thought.

Then thwack!

Everything went black.

Ian had flown into a huge tree trunk just off the ski run,
hitting it with his skis and his head. His ski helmet was no match
for the impact at that speed.

He died instantly.

The skier in the black hoodie and dark ski glasses stood in
the trees, watching from the far side of the trail. He slowly skied
away.

"Sunyata, are you there?"

It was like a strange voice in Sunyata's mind.

"I just bought the farm on the ski hill; I'm making the
transition. I skied down the wrong trail. Lost control, went up a
mogul, and launched myself into the air and right into a huge tree;
some practice run. It was all so fast. It had been such a beautiful
and exciting moment. I guess that's the way life goes.

"Please tell Caitlin I'm so sorry to leave her. Tell her to say good-bye to my kids and grandkids and, most important, that I love her forever and I'm grateful for the life we had together. Whatever you guys do, press on with the Hucomms Project. It's so important. No one else will do this. I'm so sorry …"

Ian! Ian! Sunyata couldn't call out in his mind. *I wonder how he contacted me. Where was he going? At least he died without suffering, doing something he loved. He had so much more living to do; he had Caitlin. But we don't get to decide when time is up.*

Sunyata felt a profound emptiness, like part of him was suddenly missing. *How could something be missing from nothing?* His mind cried out for the loss of Ian. *It's me standing alone—and I felt so lonely before.*

It was only later that Sunyata stopped to wonder how Ian had managed to speak to him—after he'd died. *How could he have talked with me? Where was he?*

Now I have to be in contact with Caitlin directly; maybe Ian wanted that. I'd imagined that we had an unusual connection. But he actually talked to me after his death.

Sunyata felt a shiver in his mind. *A lot of forces we don't know about*, he mused.

Chapter 28

BIG BANG

"Sunyata, it's Chi. You have caused quite a buzz at Project Phoenix. Of course, they've totally lost trust in you." She was connected via her hidden channel.

Chi, Ian's gone. He talked to me—after he died! He hit a tree on a ski hill. He gave me a message for Caitlin, asking her forgiveness for his leaving her. He encouraged us to go on to pursue the Hucomm Project. I don't know where his voice came from, but I heard it in my mind—just like I hear what you are saying. Chi, I feel like a piece of me is gone—torn out of me. How was he able to speak with me after he died? Now I'm going to have to talk with Caitlin to give her his message.

"I called Caitlin as soon as I heard; she seemed to be accepting Ian's death."

Caitlin had told Chi that, since Ian had come back from his coma, she had wondered how long she would have him with her. Ian had repeatedly reminded her that his (and all) life was transient.

She worried about his insistence on skiing. They both knew that his knee was vulnerable. He felt that he had to continue skiing to stay truly alive. He was preoccupied with the idea of living fully. She was aware that she had almost lost him before but felt the years they had together were a gift. She knew he died being Ian.

Was she devastated? Yes! Does she blame Ian? Not really. She said that he never went halfway in life—or in his love for her. Caitlin knew the risks. She would go on living her life with the same intensity as Ian had lived his.

Chi told Sunyata about her meeting with Ian and Caitlin, what a wonderful relationship they had, and then mentioned that Ian had been hearing his own thoughts echoing. "Ian had wondered if they were your thoughts he could perceive."

Sunyata wondered if the two of them had some energy connection that had allowed Ian to hear some of his similar thoughts. Perhaps the same connection had allowed Ian to communicate with him from his spirit after his death.

Chi responded that this sounded like a reasonable explanation. She was intrigued by the possibility. "Some findings in quantum physics may explain this," she said. She agreed that Sunyata should talk with Caitlin about it.

"None of us really know how much life we have left," Chi mused. "And you may have the same soul, Sunyata. Maybe that's why your thoughts intermixed—from the spirit world, whatever that might be."

What are our friends at Project Phoenix up to now that they know where I stand? What do you think they'll do about it?

"They've been worried about the religious right accepting the idea of a consciousness on a chip. You know, preserving conscious life beyond the time that God intended. Are we creating artificial human life? Do we have souls? The usual concerns. So now they want to bring Project Phoenix to the world by sending your chip, with your consciousness, back to the big bang to see God at the creation and report back. They think the religious right will buy into that and ignore the other questions. They can get rid of you but make it sound like a glorious mission."

Do they have the technology to claim they could do that?

"They have spent gazillions on the development of a system that can attain supraluminal speeds using some time warp technology where laws of physics as we know them are suspended. They call the system Time Jumper. They need another huge appropriation to finish it and figure this mission will get the support they need and get rid of you at the same time. What they're not publicizing is that the mission will take about eighty years to complete! No problem for you, Sunyata, but it will be a tricky sell. They have to tout it as an accomplishment of civilization."

Sunyata couldn't hold back, as inappropriate as it might seem. The idea of being sent away, leaving Chi to die alone, was too much for him. *Chi, when will you come and fuse with my mind on the chip?*

"Sunyata, is that a proposal?"

Yes, Chi. I love you.

"Sunyata, I feel love for you. I think I would be happy as part of our joint mind, but for now, I can be much more useful for our projects in my present role here in the material world. Can we just consider ourselves engaged?"

You're serious? Will it cause any conflict of interest?

"Not if we keep it secret."

Is the general still sniffing around?

"Sunyata, you should be ashamed. He's not a bad person. He's pretty open for being career military, but he's given up on getting me in bed and moved on to younger possibilities. He doesn't even ask me to play tennis anymore. He's about to retire, I hear."

Chi, how old are you now? I've lost track.

"Shouldn't you have figured that out before your proposal,

Sunyata?" Chi suppressed a jolt of anger, remembering that Sunyata had absolutely no sense of time passing, no experience of day or night. "I'm thirty-seven. Don't you think you should know that before you ask me to merge minds on your chip forever?" she chided.

"But let me get back to what's happening at Phoenix. They're beating on me to accomplish some successful transfers. I'm trying to hold off until Buzz Stevenson dies, of course. But now they're programming volunteers, and based on the experience with you, they're holding out the possibility of a copy, with the source mind being eligible for immediate retirement, after their 'compliance training' and the transfer. I know the technical problem but can drag my feet for a while without them knowing."

What are we going to do about Hucomms if they send me off to the Big Bang?

"Sunyata, Caitlin and I need to include your ideas in the Epstein Hucomms planning grant. Since Ian's death, Caitlin has thrown herself totally into this project and is directing the Hucomms Institute in Santa Fe and collaborating with the Santa Fe Institute that has the best minds in physics, computer technology, and theoretical mathematics. They have formed a joint committee that can be trusted. In the meantime, I'll keep in touch regarding Project Big Bang and the Phoenix II program to develop more transferred mind clones."

Good-bye, Chi. I'll look forward to our meeting soon, if they haven't unplugged me.

"Sunyata, don't worry. The DARPA boys now know that they don't have a clue about the basics underlying the transfer procedure. DARPA has total mission control, but they've had to return total technical control to me until I produce enough for them. No one at DARPA would dare even touch your biochip; they're at least aware that they don't know enough to fool with it."

Chapter 29

TIME JUMPER:
THE GRAND VOYAGE

The atmosphere was festive at the Kennedy Space Center. It was a warm spring day; the crowds at and around Kennedy were both much larger and of a different type than usually seen attending space flight launches. Many religious groups had come in mass to pray for and observe the liftoff of Time Jumper. All night vigils and prayer sessions were held in many nearby locations, including once-empty fields within a few miles of the launch site.

Division and disagreement were in the air; groups who saw this as a holy mission to save the earth and its groups who contended that God would only reveal Himself on His schedule, when humans were ready or had qualified for a return of the Messiah. Each religious group had a firm and often polarized opinion on Project Big Bang. Of course, each group was sure that God had validated its position. This led to conflict, with various religious groups opposing each other with fury; the stakes were high.

Project Big Bang was really big business, which meant it was also big politics. The budget was in the billions, which were spread around like jam to defense contractors.

Many of the fundamentalist groups were staunch supporters; they were weighing in pro or con. The fact that no one had the faintest idea what the project would produce didn't matter; people were willing to die to reach back and meet God, and some others were willing to die to prevent "an intrusion upon the Lord." Human identity and belief were on the line; for some their "raison d'être" was in play.

There it was—a modern pyramid, twenty stories tall, with five mounted rockets ten football fields in length. It came to a sharp point, about ten feet long, that was solid electronics—the brain of Big Bang. An old-fashioned cockpit was painted on the needle-shaped, lead rocket, with the words "Major Ian Farrell" painted below the lines of the cockpit that was housing the chip, representing Major Farrell to the world as the "pilot" who would faithfully relay back information during the trip. The fact that the "trip," the grand voyage, would take eighty years.to reach the Big Bang was not clearly spelled out. Instead, the masses were told to expect frequent reports of the progress of the Voyage.

That area with the major's name on a mock-up of a jet fighter cockpit was where Major Farrell, a.k.a. Sunyata, was to be placed for the grand voyage. Dr. Chi MacDonald, PhD in neurophysics, the mother of Project Phoenix, was in charge of all of the technical aspects of the move of the Project Phoenix chip to Time Jumper, a space transfer system expected to attain speeds faster than that of light, a feat deemed impossible, until very recently.

The managers of Project Phoenix were not happy entrusting

the "liberal," nonmilitary MacDonald with such responsibility, but having failed to complete another transfer since demoting her, they were fearful of another disaster they could not address. They settled for infiltrating her technical team with CIA agents to watch her. The agents had very little technical understanding of just what Dr. MacDonald was doing as she supervised the transfer of the biochip to Time Jumper.

That Major Farrell had sacrificed his body to be the traveler who would allow the rest of the world to picture God at the creation of the universe set up parallels to other divine martyrs, such as Jesus, Mohammed, and many others—despite the inconvenient fact that Major Farrell, a.k.a. Sunyata, was a determined agnostic.

But what is really more important? Reality or belief? Belief is founded on faith. Faith comes from what? A desire to believe? A conversion based on what? A promise that is accepted—with perks, if it is true. Pascal's wager—maintain faith and your ass is covered; don't buy into faith and you're on your own—means no assurances of anything! Everybody wants some assurance, even if there is none.

We're not talking about being a good humanitarian, spending your life helping others—doing the right thing. No! You must have faith and declare it! Or all bets are off.

So, Chi, in her official role, surrounded by clean-cut killing machines, took the elevator up twenty stories and, with the help of her technicians, installed the pod—a five-foot-long tubular device with a diameter of three feet containing the chip on which Major Farrell, national hero and martyr, resided.

A cheer went up; people wept with joy and anticipation—the countdown proceeded. TV coverage was minute in its detail; the world held its breath. The liftoff was massive, shooting flames from heaven, snorting steam, and releasing the forces of the gods! The grand voyage was successfully launched; of course, if God was unhappy, He would have prevented it, right? He must have welcomed it, right? Hey, but that was just the liftoff. Plenty of opportunities for God to intervene remained along the way. He could just blow up Time Jumper—anytime. Just wait!

Does God give a damn what happens to some man-made super rocket?

Does anyone really believe He cares about such things? Is He a he? How about a she, like Lakshmi? Did God spin our universe like a top and make evolution happen? Was evolution God's idea? Maybe our reality—whether we get invited to the ball, whether we die of cancer or some terrible accident—is just God's dream. Maybe we're just subjects in a grand experiment (though we don't seem to have signed an internal-review-board-approved permission).

Consider Job—a good guy, who was prospering and living a good life, following God's commandments. But then the devil and God had to have a pissing match, and Job (who was picked as the test case) was afflicted with boils and lost his family, his wealth—everything. His "friends" decided that he must have "deserved it"—must have done bad things (blame the victim).

Job got really pissed off—it wasn't fair; life wasn't fair. It just was. Job's life ended up being restored; he had withstood the test. How many Jobs do you know?

Look in the mirror. Can you stand the test without going bonkers? Is it God and the devil having a pissing contest? Or is God really the law of probability? Or maybe He just gave the top one really big spin and it's still spinning—evolution and all.

After the launch, Chi returned to her lab by Blackhawk. Everyone congratulated each other (after all, what they had just accomplished had made their careers). Some even had a few shots of Irish whiskey. Chi smiled, drank a couple toasts to the future of Big Bang and Phoenix, and disappeared to her laboratory to "check something out." People were used to Chi doing that. During her entire career, Chi had always gone her own way, and people had learned to accept that.

Sunyata reflected on all that had occurred over the past few days, smiling as he thought of Chi's brilliance. She had installed special relays from the Time Jumper in his tetra-biochip. These relay devices would allow Sunyata to report data "from the mission" via his chip, which was safe, hidden on the ground in an obscure laboratory four stories below the desert.

Chi had developed a cadre of technicians, fiercely loyal to her, who had installed the sensors (instead of what was thought to be the tetra-biochip) in Time Jumper. Installing a series of relays allowed Chi to safely hide Sunyata's chip without detection. No one save Chi would know with certainty that Sunyata still had a home in the crowded laboratory as Time Jumper roared back in time.

As far as the unknowing "intelligence" officers who were monitoring the installation of Sunyata's tetra-biochip into the Time Jumper system could tell, Sunyata was gone on a journey to the big bang that would take eighty years, if Time Jumper didn't self-destruct before then. Now that DARPA, using new "personality screens," had successfully transferred other recruits to chips, they were quite happy to be "rid of" the temperamental Sunyata, who could not be counted on to "follow orders."

Sunyata reflected. *More triumphs for science and technology. A new era of advances in "robotic warfare" has dawned; increasingly, no humans will have to do the dangerous and dirty work of killing. It is now "sanitized," with "desk warriors" essentially playing "war games" from monitors in the United States. The warriors now "work" from nine to five, wiping out terrorists with controlled robots with the ability to navigate any terrain and a destructive capacity from lasers and explosives that are awesome.*

At least our young are not coming home with body parts blown off or traumatic brain injuries. They are at an office, sitting at their monitors controlling armies of robots, while eating potato chips and texting home. Such progress! How could those primitive terrorists dedicated to the destruction of Western civilization even stay in the game?

The nuclear cat was long out of the bag; it was only a question of time. What other direction did these people now have?

Can we use science to improve our warfare methods with a steep enough curve to vanquish a world, producing people who have no direction other than terrorism? If you get to a point where you are willing to die to find meaning in your miserable life, why shouldn't you blow yourself up for your cause? Why not take a chance on an afterlife of willing virgins? Anybody got a better deal?

This is what we had come to—warfare that was technologically "clean"—massive destructiveness from a distance, focused by robotics, against insurgent movements where crude hydrogen weapons are ineffective. The higher up, the farther away from the bloody grime, the easier wreaking havoc on others is. Death at a distance—remarkable! It was just like a video game—like make-believe. Ah, the wonder of progress! And we can make tons of money, money, money from it. The better the weapons, the more they cost—a formula for wealth creation.

God's law of evolution—the fittest survive (and prosper). That's Gods Law all right! The Devil takes the hindmost.

More and more money will be spent (and made) on defense. We will leave our enemies with no real alternative—either they must attempt to become more destructive or they will face miserable lives of meaninglessness.

Where is this leading us? A civilized world, clawing for more materials and schadenfreude and a lower world that has no alternative but to destroy what they hate—each pursuing increasing levels of destruction.

We're going off the fucking tracks! Can humanity survive in its present form? As long as we can defer the cost to the next generation, we can stumble along—gorging all the way—whistling "after me, the deluge" or "technology will solve the problems." Our new god— technology. But for how many generations will this last?

We live for such a short time that we have no concept of time; the profit next quarter will make me rich! Our world is a series of images; we have lost the concept of linearity.

Make my killing and get out.

He who dies with the most toys wins!

Humanity is headed for extinction. Do you care? Or do you gorge, while you can? Eat, drink, and be merry, for tomorrow—

"Sunyata, you okay? We've been attaching things and moving you round a bit.

"Time Jumper has left with sensors aboard that you and Magna will have to monitor. The country is up in arms; you are a hero—and they and the DARPA boys seem convinced you are riding Time Jumper. It is still soaring upward and outward. The new supraluminal system isn't scheduled to 'fire' for eight hours."

I was just thinking about the future of humanity and technology. Chi, I also want to tell you that I had no business asking you to join me with your mind on my chip. It isn't fair; it was so selfish of me. You're a young woman with so much life to live. I want you with me forever, but I'm sorry I made that demand on you.

"Sunyata, I'm a big girl. I can make mature decisions for myself. I have thought about my life. You know, of course, that material life is not as important for me as full consciousness."

We have lots of time to think about it and talk about it. In the meantime, I will make love to you in my thoughts—and maybe we can find new ways to share our love.

"Sunyata, with your imagination and my determination, we'll explore many ways to share our love.

"I'm going to find a way to secretly get your chip moved over to the Hucomms Project, which has recently completed a huge facility for development. Once you are safely moved and I know the chain of command there and we have the transfer system working, we can decide how to be together. I've been notified that I'll be retired to consultant status, now that Phoenix has some new transfers."

Chi, you've managed this situation very successfully, and you are right to get everything settled in advance. I can't wait to get moved over to the Hucomms Project. If you decide to transfer to this chip, it will be another step in the development of Hucomms. By the way, whatever happened to Buzz Stevenson? Did he get his transfer?

"You couldn't think that I would allow such a grossly narcissistic person on a chip, if I had any control. I just kept dragging my feet; the DARPA managers were getting suspicious and had begun to confront me about the delay, but I held on just long enough. Your 'force' probability came through. He developed new metastases of his prostate cancer, became depressed, and shot himself. Everyone was relieved—no one considered him a good candidate for a transfer. But he had the clout to get it done."

I'm not surprised. He was such an empty person—not someone well equipped to deal with things not going well, despite his intelligence. No real attachments to anyone else. Sad ... Chi, if and when you decide to make the transfer, who will be in charge of the Hucomms Project?

"Caitlin, Skip, and their team of course."

24030915R00113

Made in the USA
Lexington, KY
02 July 2013